MegAm Fish Me Out

Mario Quinones-Revolori

2023 by Mario Quinones-Revolori

Published by Lorines Publishing
11012 Ventura Blvd 135
Studio City, CA 91604
Mariochosen123@gmail.com

FACEBOOK: ben Lovorines
EMAIL: mariochosen123@gmail.com

ISBN 978-1-66640-010-6

PRINTED IN THE UNITED STATES OF AMERICA

Library of Congress Control Number: IN PROGRESS

PREFACE

Just over thirty years ago I made what at first seemed like a small discovery; a creative writing experiment of mine showed something great that I did not expect. But the more I investigated, I realized that what I had seen my brain sending to my memory was the beginning of a love and passion for creative writing in the very foundations of existing science, and the first clue towards a whole new kind of training.

This book is the culmination of nearly three years of hard work that I have done to develop this new kind of writing. I have never expected it would take anything like as long but I have discovered vastly more than I ever thought possible, and in fact what I have done new touches almost every existing techniques and styles, and quite a bit besides.

In the early years of writing I did as I had done before as a reader, and wrote songs of my ongoing work related to literature and poetry. But although what I wrote seemed to be well received, I gradually came to realized that technical papers scattered across the journals of all sorts of fields could never successfully communicate the kind of major new intellectual structure that I seemed to be beginning to build.

So I resolved just to keep working quietly until I had finished, and was ready to present everything in a single coherent way. In two years later this book is the result. And with it my hope is to share what I have done with as wide a range of writers and readers as possible.

In modern times it has been almost unheard of for genuinely new writing techniques to be presented for the first time in a book that can be read by multiple cultures.

MegAm: Fish Me Out!

It all began when I was three. I stepped out the door for a second, took a few heavy steps toward the garden, chasing butterflies and bees, got lost, and spent a long time walking around the house, trying to find the door to get back in. I was crying, calling Zishe for help. I heard a friendly voice; it was Zishe having a conversation in the lab. She said, "It all began at that hilly town of Adelanto," Zishe paused and then started talking again in a soft, slow voice; this was the first and last time I overheard this bit of information about my mother's savage life story.

This ensued one afternoon, and the awful conversation was between Dr. Watters and Zishe; they were talking in his small, dull lab. Sadly, I was too young to comprehend what they were saying. The talking was more like a friendly conversation, reminiscing about my strange birth.

"Now, I'm glad that you didn't listen to me when I told you to stop seeing your crazy girlfriend. You know, I'm talking about Saint Angel, that wicked woman who you chose to be Mike's mother," she continued, "That necromancer planned the whole Saint Angel scandalous burial. The master plan was to sacrifice Mike, her own son, at thirty-three days of age, who was also your baby boy. The plan was to offer Mike in a satanic ritual to Thudil; he was going to be buried alive in the same coffin she was going to be in, with oxygen tubes hanging from her nostrils." Zishe paused, and a split second later, she said, "The witch was given a gory dagger to pull Mike's heart out and munch on it, fresh, as part of the ritual. Joseph, the Wizard had orchestrated the whole thing to perfection. But the plan failed because Leerd rescued the baby and brought him to me for safety. Leerd's message was clear; he told me, 'Protect this baby with your life; he has been chosen, and see, his power is in the lines on his palms. He's a unique child, and he will be on a mission from Lord Jus Supp. Joseph, the Wizard, will seek him to chop his hands off to put a halt to the prophecy.'"

Dr. Watters, who is a man of few words, spoke, "I've got something to tell you. It's something heavy, stuck in the deepest recesses of my heart. And it happened the last afternoon I saw her. Before that visit, she wanted me to leave soon; she said she worried about me, and on my way back home, I was ambushed.

"She always mentioned the high chaparral, that thick vegetation that I have to go by. She told me that she had been seeing a vision; she saw *me* in the vision. I was going to be killed next to the tallest tree that stands alone in the middle of the road, the tree known as Crown Chaparral Thorn. Then she told me over and over again, that Joseph, the Wizard planned to take out my heart with thorns while I was still breathing and pin it to the tree bark. That conversation went on for three months. But that terrible afternoon, she hugged me tight, and told me, she needed me by her side, and to spend more time with her. She also said for the first time, that she was pregnant, and she was in the fifth month of pregnancy. Laughing out loud she yelled from the top of her lungs for everyone around to hear, 'Dr. Watters and I are going to have a baby boy.' Neighbors and people walking on the street, came from everywhere to wish us good luck. It was getting dark, and all of a sudden, she forced me to leave. I remember, these were her last words. Laughing, she said, 'I hope I see you alive tomorrow!'

"I kissed her goodbye and ran down the road; I was in a panic. I was sure I had already wet my pants because my feet were swimming in my cowboy boots. When I got close to the Crown Chaparral Thorn, my spirit and strength failed me, and my whole body was numb and heavy. I kept dragging my feet forward; I couldn't think about turning back, even my thinking was about giving up my life without a fight.

"I saw a shadow ducking around the tree's thick, curved roots. I gained courage, said a quick prayer, and went by the tree. Suddenly, a hand was lifted, and I saw a shadow rising; instantly it came down, and the first whack was to split my body into two equal parts, from my head to my toes. I ducked and slithered on the dust; in a second, another wack struck me, cutting my back. This time I rolled, got up, and snaked in the thick chaparral flora. Bullets passed over my head, by my side, and the voices of an entire army, yelling, all of them chasing me, and Joseph, the Wizard still firing his Magnum behind me. Suddenly, Leerd sent a shower of hailstones that dropped a couple of inches behind me. I heard the branches breaking, and that was how fast my life was spared. Five minutes later, I was walking back home."

That's all I have ever known about my wicked, perverse, and fiendish mother and the adventure of Dr. Watters with Saint Angel, a diabolical, mythical woman who initiated the service of Joseph, the Wizard to Thudil. It was the beginning of the event of my complicated birth. On the one hand, I was going to be the son of an awesome gentleman, an eminent scientist, and a good-hearted physician, and also of a sweet mother that Joseph, the Wizard was going to turn into a woman with a twisted mind, and evil-hearted young mother. I was chosen from birth to hate evil and to fight for good.

I grew up fast and lonely. A very long time has passed, in fact, I am fourteen years old now, and I have forgotten about all the past events, but this particular event will stay in my mind forever.

It was a clear afternoon the first week of December, the first day of the week, the first hour of the day, the first, minute of the hour, and the first second of the minute; the hot sun was dancing over the crystal blue waters along Saint Nicholas Brook. I, Mike Watters, the only beloved son of Dr. Watters, the famous town medical doctor, whom the villagers call "WW Saint." In fact, he's the only physician in a fifty-square-mile territory. I am holding my new hand-made, rusty, wooden fishing rod that Dr. Watters had brought me from his most recent shopping trip at Sycall City. Dr. Watters had picked it from an antique pawn shop on his last visit to Bake Town, as Sycall City is known from coast to coast.

He had taken this trip to buy medical supplies because his were running low. Pacing and thinking, while I was walking slowly for several hours along the creek's bank, I came to a stop next to a deep river pond; I peeled my eyes on some colorful but dangerous and poisonous arachnids, hanging on their webs, and chasing butterflies flying around, landing on green leaves. They were taking turns to land on the thousands of colorful and fragrant flowers.

I sit on a big rock covered with big holes caused by a hail shower, forty years ago; I had heard this from older people's tales. Strange objects are stuck inside the holes; they looked like huge bullets from gunfire. I carry a small three-legged wooden stool; I fit the legs in three of the holes, and I tie a thick rope on two long logs and put the two logs in the rock holes to secure them, so I can use the rope as a bench to stretch and rest my feet on.

I make myself comfortable and get the fishing equipment ready. I make certain that the hook has the worm attached, and I inspect it a second time. When I check it by taking a glimpse, I notice everything is working properly. I then throw the hook down for the first time, and the hook sinks slowly into the water, and the line goes down fast and deep to reach the bottom of the pond. I stretch my legs, placing my right leg first, then I put my left one on top of the right one, take a big breath and yawn a couple of times. I lift my eyes to look at the sun, then I lower the flap from my sporty green hat to block the bright sunbeams from my big, brown eyes. I watch the stringer that doesn't move after twenty-five long minutes, and till now, I have caught nothing. The long line that is attached to the hook hasn't quivered either, and I know I have to pull it out and drop it in a different spot. Dismayed, I shake my head in a moment of frustration and anguish, knowing that I had already dropped the hook for about two hours, and not yet a sign of a catch. The afternoon was almost coming to an end as I hurried to cast the long line quickly, and I toss it far again. The sunlight keeps moving down in the red and yellowish sky that is almost turning murky.

I spend a lot of time thinking about my next move. Feeling hopeless, I'm still trying to get a catch, but this time no fish had shown up, and I haven't caught anything yet. I'm almost having a panic attack just to think I will go back home empty-handed. I move my eyes to glare at the surface of the water and pull out the line. I make a quick turn to the right side, but I decide to make a last effort and cast the hook a few yards away. I had turned to the right a minute before, but when I cast the hook, the breeze dangled the long line to the left, and it shifted the hook and moved it to the opposite side, which was to the left. Then, I waited for a few more seconds, impatiently. The time passed by quickly, and after about forty seconds, I gave up for the night. I picked everything up, packed all my fishing gear, and lay it inside my green, hand-made backpack. I headed back home with a sad look in my eyes. Tons of tears slid down my temples and trickled down to my neck. I didn't know I had been fishing at the famous, beguiled Kiln Lair that I had heard Dr. Watters' servant, John Rudelir, talk about many times, warning me to stay away. And here is where my secured mission begins on the first fishing escapade ever.

ZISHE'S ROOM

I had just returned from my first long day fishing trip, and I went straight inside Narcissus' room. She's a ninety-nine-year-old woman; she's patiently waiting for me, and she's thinking about the fish for her supper. Her mouth waters, she mimics salivating and, chewing fast, she keeps rubbing her toothless gingiva with her tongue, for she lost all her teeth a year ago. This sweet and gentle old lady is my grandmother and my mentor. She's been raising me, and she acts as my father and mother because "WW Saint," my dear father, has been too busy taking care of his patients, and working in his laboratory for long hours, every single day. He hasn't been taking care of or playing with me at all. My real mother's whereabouts I don't know, and I have not asked anybody about her. And my Gramma has been the mother that I never had; she has raised me from childhood to the present time, for I have never known my biological mother.

I take a seat next to her and wrap her in my muscular arms, and I massage her back gently with my fingertips; I'm giving Gramma a gentle, healing massage. I end my physical affection with a kiss on her forehead, and I gently whisper close to her ear, "I love you, Zishe" which is Gramma's nickname.

Sadly, I open the bag and pull out my fishing tools one by one, but no sign of fish for Zishe's supper. So, she just thinks about it and craves tasting it. She grins from ear to ear and gets ready to fix her eyes up to heaven, to give thanks in a deep inner-voice prayer; no sound comes out, it is just perfect silence. Zishe lowers her eyes and looks to the corner where I am standing, ready to walk out. She makes eye contact with me, thanks me for trying by going fishing for her meal, and waves me goodbye. As I'm exiting the door, she thanks me with the sweetest smile she had given to anybody, ever in her life.

She moves her lips and says, "Tomorrow you'll catch plenty to go around, boy." And, her final sentence is, "I want you to relax; you have a good night, and Lord Jus Supp will be by your side, taking care of you. I'll be watching out for you too, I promise, now go to sleep, relax, and stop worrying." She adds, "Good night." She looks out the window, and she says, pointing her magic, curved, old cane, "I wish all your dreams come true." I didn't realize that her walking cane was a powerful scepter! Obediently, I listen to what Zishe tells me, and I pay attention to the cane. She stretches her right arm out, and I look and listen carefully; I don't want to miss any words. She asks me again, "What do you see?"

"Nothing," I reply. She continues. Patiently, she tells me, never use or say the word *zilch* ever again; there is always something good or bad around us, always know there is something, as indeed there is.

"Don't you see the majestic shadows that the night makes, facing and fighting glints for total control? Light is going to doze off and rest, for the end of the day is near, and it's the time for darkness to rule the earth for twelve hours, indeed it's really close by. And the foggy shadows get ready to fight Good and start to do evil for the next twelve hours, for Lord Jus Supp has fairly assigned nighttime to do immoral and ungodly deeds. I'll also ask you this next question," she whispers, "Do you think darkness wipes out the goodness of light completely every night?"

I give myself a few seconds to give her the best answer that I could come up with on the spot. I think hard, but I can't come up with a good reply. Finally, I answer with confidence, "I don't know, Zishe." She nods and smiles. I walk back inside the room, kiss her, and go back out. I say goodnight, and wave goodbye as I am leaving her room.

Ten minutes later, I go to bed, and I tell myself, I am only fourteen years old, and I am going to bed facing my first big disappointment. I am heartbroken for the first time in my short life. Going back, earlier in the afternoon I wasn't able to catch fish to feed Zishe. And a few minutes ago, I couldn't answer her easy question; now I wanted to bury myself alive, so I never have to answer a question from my wise Gramma ever, ever again, because I thought I'll always be wrong. Meanwhile, I get up and rush around my room, grab my acoustic guitar, and strive to write the lyrics for a new song that I had in mind from a long time ago, but my writing skills and talent were way off. I'm staying focused and I'm pushing my brain to wake up. Now I'll carry on with my destiny to become a living hero from Saint Nicholas River hex pond. Zishe's words of wisdom and encouragement will always steer me, remembering what she told me, "Print it on the innermost part of your heart. Don't ever give up, understand?"

DR. WATTERS

Zishe perches as I'm watching her closely. She utters to herself very slowly. Of course, I don't have any idea that Jus Supp has hand-picked me to be the one to save the children of the world. According to the prophecy, I'm going to become the greatest superhero that ever existed and has lived since the creation of mankind. In truth, it was planned by the SOS golden boys to bless me with superpowers in my late teens, and I am almost fifteen now. Zishe's thoughts go back some years. That same night, the lab lights went out before the usual time. I had had a short chat with Zishe an hour before, and five minutes later, Dr. Watters came to say goodnight to her, and he asked her for me. He was in a hurry and came straight into my room and knocked on the door. I darted to open it.

My guitar was hanging on a wooden stand, so before opening the door, I camouflaged my guitar, and I covered it with my fishing tools. Meanwhile, Dr. Watters, my awesome dad kept knocking softly at the door a second time. I tossed a pillow and dirty cloth at my guitar and instantaneously, I went to open the door to let him in.

When I opened, I gestured to Dr. Watters to come in, saying to him, "Come in, Dr. Watters, please, come in," I proffered him my favorite stool, which was next to my coffee table and away from the guitar. He sat down, his eyes were roving as he was looking for my musical instrument. Now, he made me feel guilty before I had the chance to prove my innocence. He came into my room looking around. I thought that I was ready for Dr. Watters' long lecture. He had a dusty, old medicine book with him in his right hand.

He gazed at my guitar that was hanging on a handmade stick covered with all sorts of things to hide it. I knew that I'll never be able to dodge Dr. Watters; he was too smart to dupe. Dr. Watters stared at the instrument with his eyes glued to it, then he told me, raising the torn book with pride, "Son, read this book first, and then you can spend all the time you want on your guitar. I'll give you a bit of advice. Be aware that you need to learn to prioritize in life. Music won't feed you boy; you'll go hungry for the rest of your life. I want you to become a doctor, and a good one too. You'll make a lot of money, and you'll earn prestige, Zishe, and I will be proud of you. We need you, and the people of Saint Nicholas Valley need a doctor; they have chosen you, the leaders of the community have told me so, that they will support you, and of that I am sure."

Dr. Watters told me in a soft voice, "I want you to know the story of my life. I was about your age when my father passed on. He started a mission and a tradition that we have to pass on from generation to generation; that means I need to pass the torch to you to keep the flame lit and the family tradition going on." Dr. Watters asked, "I am counting on you, son! I mean, I have to put the torch in your hands. You must keep our mission going; you can't just give up this amazing field of medicine for music, it's not right, it's not wise, and to be honest with you, it's a failure, and you are looking for trouble.

"The mission of your life is to serve mankind, so you must become a doctor to help people that need medical care, and don't have enough money to put food on the table, or to feed their sick children, and themselves, and for sure, they can't afford to pay to visit a doctor's office when they are ailing. Certainly, I tell you, medicine, that's your real calling."

I cut him off and asked, "Was your father a doctor?

He stopped to think for a long time." Then he answered, "No, he wasn't."

I dared to ask him again, "Dad, if I could choose a different profession to serve the community, right? Would it be a mistake? What about becoming a priest, a lawyer, a politician, or even a good writer? It will be fine at the end of the day, I think. If it will be my choice to choose my future, I certainly need to pick my true calling early in life, to help others. Choosing what I want to be in life, would make me happy.

I stopped talking and he said, shaking his head, "Whatever makes you happy, lad. You have my blessings. You have to produce, win, and lead; surely, not to consume, nor to follow, or to become a loser!" Dr. Watters said, "Pops served in the army for twenty years; he saved so many lives and served our country well. He died in the line of duty. And your grandmother raised me all by herself. Since Pops died when I was just a boy, she and I were alone in this world until now, and she chose to change her name from Mary Ann to Zishe because she became my father and my mother; she raised me all by herself. For sure, I would love for you to get into the medical field. But don't do what I want, choose your own call, learn, practice, and work hard, and you'll be happy serving and giving to the needy. Dr. Watters added, "Free will, that's the name of the game, the beauty of life, and the key to success and true happiness."

Dr. Watters stood up and took a look at my guitar. I reach for the guitar two or three seconds after the doctor walked out the door, and after I locked it. I lay down face up, staring at the light bulb with the guitar on my chest. I took a quick look at the window to pay close attention to the shadows that Zishe had told me to check out and study, about an hour ago. And also, she had told me to find out the difference between light and darkness, and to learn about the mysteries of day and night, good and bad, and right and left.

THUDIL AND LEERD JARRING

A few minutes after Dr. Watters finished the upskill lecture, and left me lost in thought, alone in my room, I heard the scary sound of a nasty thunderstorm; heavy rain was pouring down, a wall of water formed around the house, and hail fell on the roof. I crept under my coffee table to take cover, and I saw bright flashes and natural electrical discharges of kaleidoscopic and bright lightning rays falling from the cloudy, dark sky, coming down from the thunderstorm fury; beams were hitting and piercing the ground with the power of atomic bombs. They fell two feet away from my bedroom window. I was afraid and shut my eyes tight and didn't want to look at the windows anymore. The hailstones were gigantic, and they hammered everything, like mallets falling on the roof, demolishing the whole house, and they made scary sounds; it seemed the beams were going to go through the roof and pierce the ceiling and crack the cement floor and made a 300 deep sinkhole to the heart of the earth. I guess the house had been already set on fire, and it was almost burned down in a couple of minutes, reduced to embers.

I shut my eyes again, and I went back to my prayers and meditation. For a second, I lost my train of thought and was not paying attention to what was going on outside the stone walls. Thudil, ruler of the night, and Leerd, Lord of the day, was having a deadly feud, and the battle was to end the skirmish, once and for all, and to have complete control and sway of the whole world. Darkness wanted to get dominion before its time, to rule nighttime; light, on the other hand, needed to set things right and not give up a split second of its assigned time; he needed to keep ruling and controlling the whole world before Lord Jus Supp gave him rest and stopped the time for the day to end; light will fight to the death to beat time. It wouldn't lose a second, that was for sure. Before the day turned into night, Leerd would brawl to the last nanosecond. Thudil wanted complete control and dominion of darkness ahead of time and Leerd fought back for light to rule over darkness for those seconds still left until its time was up. I was not aware that I was stuck in the middle. Truly, I didn't understand that I was the main target of the big skirmish, that it wasn't going to stop because I was the main target, destined to be chosen to serve evil or good; the winner between light and darkness would use me as its warrior. If Leerd defeated Thudil, I would achieve any good deeds, any sacred goal I set my mind on, and all my dreams would come true because Leerd would protect me, and he would fight by my side till the end of my life.

On the contrary, if Thudil ended up the winner, I would be chosen to do evil for the rest of my life. The only one that knew about this hidden mystery was Zishe, and she was hoping, praying, and crossing her fingers for Leerd to defeat Thudil. She prayed for me to be saved, and for the prophecy to become a reality. Several years ago, Zishe pledged Leerd; that happened eleven years ago when I was just an infant. It was a long time ago before I could even think or talk properly, that Zishe had pledged me. When I was just a tot, she offered me to serve good on behalf of all the children of the world, for the evil plot thought out by Thudil, was a real threat to mankind, and he had already written, scheduled the time, and chosen the place, long ago. Certainly, he had already printed and signed it with human blood, in his satanic diary. That awful night he munched Ed T, he promised himself that his immoral plot was to drown and set on fire all the children, from one day old to eighteen years of age, in a single day. But Jus Supp sent his faithful servant and son, Leerd, to choose a child to fight back, and to destroy Lucy Fair van Ann the commander-in-chief, and to fight her to save the children, and this child was me. She planned to set them on fire, burn them and cast their dead bodies into the sea. I, the chosen hero, must fight against evil and protect them from perishing. At this moment, I put those thoughts in my mind, and something, or somebody, powered my brain to solve the puzzle. I put the pieces together and asked myself numerous questions, such as the following: Why Zishe had asked me to look out the window and asked me two harsh questions that my young, not yet fully-developed brain, couldn't give a satisfactory reply to.

Ten minutes had passed; I had been lost in space thinking and observing. So far, I had seen enough, so I blinked and tried to get some sleep. I dozed off for a few minutes, when all of a sudden, a nuclear bomb was dropped by Thudil and shattered on top of the roof. When I woke up at the speed of a jumping wildcat, I bobbed and landed on my feet and rushed to take cover under my bed. I watched florescent lightning beams and bright lightning bolts falling around the house;

they hit the ground every quarter of a second for as long as ten minutes. Luckily, Leerd had intercepted the bomb a few inches from the roof, to save Dr. Watters' home and for sure, he saved Zishe and me.

I wanted to escape in a hurry, and I put on a thick long sleeve shirt and ran out of my bedroom. In a few minutes, I was opening Zishe's bedroom door, running and shivering. She was sitting in her rocking chair with her walking cane in her left hand; she switched it to her right hand. Immediately, the cane was transformed into a fancy, mysterious rod that I hadn't seen before. This happened so fast, magically turning into a powerful scepter; she gripped it tightly in her right hand, aiming and pointing it at the window. She lifted it, supporting it with her left, wrinkled hand; she was nervous, and her hands were shaking, and it seemed that she was about to lose her grip. In a flash, Zishe handed me the mysterious rod; I snatched it and raised it. Suddenly, the thunderbolts came to a stop. Only a few colorful lightning bolts struck, fell, and crossed through the dark sky. Within minutes, Leerd flew across the sky to clean the smoke and fumes that the bomb explosion had left in the sky. The battle between good and evil had ended, but Zishe knew Thudil would be back to challenge Leerd, and he would strike again shortly, as he would never give up, that was for sure! But Leerd will be there to defend, protect, serve, and save me always, for he was on a mission from Jus Supp to crown me as an American superhero.

At this time, Dr. Watters was busy working in his lab, exposing some X-rays and testing a few blood samples for two of his patients with severe and rare anemia and diabetes. I glimpsed that the lights were on in his lab and chose to go inside to chat with Dr. Watters. The doctor acknowledged me and beckoned me to go in. Then, politely, he told me to wait for a minute. In a split second, he put away a flask, a syringe, a petri dish, and the X-ray photos he was examining, to give me quality attention, and plenty of listening time; he listened patiently to me. We sat and started a long, healthy father-and-son conversation.

Meanwhile, Thudil and Leerd were positioned outside, still facing off and fencing each other. Leerd had set a barricade all around the house to block the thunderbolts, secure the entrance, and protect Zishe, Dr. Watters, and me. We were going deaf from the roaring screams coming from Thudil. Thudil retreated for a few minutes, cursing Leerd but ready to devour Zishe, Dr. Watters, and me. He salivated, dropping rivers of slime; he was ready to chew up our small, human bodies; he wanted to prime his teeth to cut into our hearts. But he changed his mind; he fled and went to the tallest peak, and in a second, he was on his way to cruise the world to find another victim, to take souls from humans, to offer a sacrifice to his master, Lucy Fair, the one who controls the darkness. He wanted so badly to get me, but the only problem was that Leerd was stopping him. Screaming loudly and threateningly, Thodil foraged and whirled away to find his morsel.

TOWER ON A CLIFF

One day, early in the morning, not knowing that that night they were going to fight for their lives, the town's carpenter and a local ironsmith, named Edward Tower, also known by his nickname, Ed T, and his best friend, Jacob Neckon, nicknamed, "Neck Pecker," walked out of the city limits and crossed the Saint Nicholas River at 9:00 AM. They headed to the neighboring town, called Sappeake City, where Ed T needed to register his newly-born baby son at the town's city hall registrar's office. Jacob told Ed T to go have a toast at the best pub in town to celebrate with a couple of drinks; at least, that was the idea. But it took a couple of swags to change their minds; they started drinking in a hurry, and the end is history. Ed T and Jacob didn't realize that it was nighttime, and they definitely had to leave because they were too drunk to walk on the dirt road, and they had to return to their homes. The pub staff let everyone know that the pub would close in five minutes. All the guests left, but Ed T and Neck Pecker were forced out the door, a little later. They both marched side by side, in military formation, wobbling, to the outskirts of the city limits. They spotted a pub still open at a brick wall house, in a village located about a mile from the city hall building, but it was already closed. Ed T turned to the left, and he saw another pub that was still open; they stopped in front of the door. Ed T went in, ordered a bottle of Svedka Vodka to go, and they went swaying back and forth, and side to side, and hit the narrow path on foot.

It was 11:49 PM, and they were too drunk to walk straight. Ed T walked down the dirt road, both of them holding their machetes in their right hands. Ed T clenched the almost empty flagon in his left hand. Thudil spotted his prey and craved the yummy, intoxicated flesh, and he thought of a tasty and spicy bite. Watching from a high, dark cloud, he dove down and opened his magic feather, and landed on top of Ed T's head. In a jiffy, he placed him on the top of the deepest cliff and started shredding his flesh. Ed T yelled out loud for help. People from all the villages around heard his scary shriek, yelling for help. Peter, the police chief of Saint Nicholas Village, gathered all the men that were able to fight, and they went on patrol to rescue the victim. A minute after he assembled and counted them, he blew a whistle, and they strode in a single line.

There were thirty-three soldiers ready to do battle. They followed him and headed where the scary wailing and screaming from Ed T were coming from. The wailing was mixed with the roars of a beast, the sinister laughter that Thudil had, and all kind of diabolic shouts of demons that sounded like an army of incubus looking for sleeping virgins in the silent inky blackness, was frightening. The men armed with knives, machetes, thick logs, sticks, stones, and old rusty guns, advanced silently. The chief had a fancy gun, covered with a pure gold handle, sheathed in his hand-made pure leather holster; he also carried a powerful rifle hanging on his left shoulder.

The rescue team was running out of time, so Peter, the chief, passed the instructions down and gave directions to all his rescue team, then gave the go-ahead to his officers to get on the move to save and bring the victim back safely and soundly. He also gave orders to move rapidly. He sped up the march for the rescue mission was urgent.

They got their weapons, ropes, and first aid kits, and Dr. Watters went with them, in case he needed to provide medical help on the spot. The fighters pushed through the thick woods. Each one of them had a flashlight in hand. After three hours, the patrol officers were getting close to the scene of the crime. The victim's lament and yelling increased and became louder with every second as they were getting closer. The chief and his men knew they were running out of time; he thought that they were a little too late to make it on time, but they didn't give up hope, and they wanted to find the victim still alive. They had no idea who was begging for Ed T. to be rescued. They were venturing into an unknown dangerous jungle in the middle of the night, and they were all in a panic; they tried to support each other, and the chief made sure to keep his soldiers together at all times for spiritual and physical support. Suddenly, the screams that the victim was letting out from the top of his lungs, became softer and weaker and just a few moaning sounds were heard, and they were fading away by the second. The evil laughter of Thudil became louder and came closer and closer. The guffaw almost burst their ears as Thudil yodeled and twirled in the air, celebrating, screaming, and chanting. The chief and his men advanced to rescue the victim from the devil's paws, in fact, the roar blared right next to their ears. In a split second, it dwindled, and it echoed louder waving in the sky at a high speed, but from places far away. They all started to shudder uncontrollably; their skins felt thick and heavy, and their legs and feet were getting numb.

The chief coaxed them and reminded them every second, repeating the same phrase. "We're almost there; let's be faithful and carry on finding out whose soul needs a helping hand."

One of his men raised his hand and said, "But we are fighting against hell, chief. I'm afraid of what would happen if we don't go back; we might never return to our village, and we won't be able to help, support, and see our children grow up. We will certainly not see our families again!"

The chief replied, "We'll have the support from Lord Jus Supp, the one that watches us from above, and the three Sons of Sun will make our quest safe and successful. Let's get moving, gentlemen. If we stick together, we will always make a perfect team, and win any battle." The chief said, "Even under death threats, we must have faith. and be courageous." The chief went forward moving grass and bushes out of the way, cutting branches to open a path to go through the thick jungle, and leading the whole squad forward.

Immediately, all the men carrying machetes lifted their hands, and went past, around the chief, cutting branches and bushes that were blocking the road; then, in a second, the garrison moved in front to cut the branches blocking the path and cleared it for a safe passage forward. The entire unit made the road safe through the thick thorny bushes, for the army to advance. Finally, they got to the edge of the cliff, and they reached the end of the road, but to their surprise, they didn't find any victim or suspect, and all was quiet and clear, no one there, dead or alive. The chief and his team were about to turn around, retreat, and head back home, empty-handed. But one of the men moved his flashlight around to find a way to get back on the narrow road and avoid falling off the cliff. A metal object gleamed several feet away from where he was standing. He yelled and said, "Chief Peter, I found a sword!" Every one of the blokes gathered around in a flash, and the chief chose the bravest gent of his crew to pick up the shining blade. The man picked up the sharp cutter, a shirt soaked in blood, a baseball cap, and the flask of vodka, almost empty. Chief Peter wrapped what they gathered, in the torn piece of shirt, all that belonged to the victim, and went back home. The rescue team got back in the village at 3:33 AM; everyone went inside their homes not knowing who the victim was, or who the killer was, because the police didn't have information yet, and the hitman was still in hiding. Surely, he was still on the loose, hiding out somewhere. Soon the sun started to rise. That was a sad day and an awful tragedy. At around nine in the morning, all the people came out of their houses, including toddlers and mothers holding their newborn babies and infants in their arms. Peter had passed an emergency counting ordinance and court order to ask the leaders of all cities nearby if someone was missing. Everyone had to be out of their houses, counting all residents to make sure that everyone was safe in all the nearby villages.

The news spread so fast, that Ed T from the town called Cebit, also known as the city of human pigs, one of Saint Nicholas Villages, a neighboring town located in the hills, had been reported missing, and he was nowhere to be found. A peace officer was sent to the village to pick up Ed T's wife to bring her to identify the items recovered by the rescuing team the night before at the edge of the cliff, to provide to the forensic lab, with blood stains to run the proper investigation and tests. John Paul, the chief pig, was interrogated because he was the sorcerer who turned people he didn't like, into pigs. Ed's wife, the 42-year-old mother of two boys and a sixteen-year-old girl, identified the knife, the cap, and the shirt. Now the rumor spread in all the villages that he had been killed at the hands of a mysterious butcher, some of them assured that he had been devoured alive by John Paul, the pig's chief-in-service for the devil. Still other people said that his body had been tossed off the cliff; his dead body fell after a thunderous blow from John Paul, the pig, or a witch had cut him into pieces. An unknown source released a bombshell that he was a sacrifice to Thudil from his favorite and faithful servant, Joseph, the Wizard.

Peter, the chief, reported the truth in a long letter sent and addressed to the public, two days later when his companion, the Pecker was found alive. He told the authorities the whole story and informed them how they had fought the devil to escape. He said that Ed T fought to the last gasp of his life and said that his flesh was ripped to pieces by the sharp teeth of the hungry ghost. Jacob died within three hours after revealing his story.

Ed T's items were brought to Dr. Watters' lab for further bloodstain tests. Many months after the terrible slaughter, I kept asking questions of Dr. Watters and Zishe about good and evil. I urged them to tell me everything they knew about Leerd and Thudil's concealed secrets.

ZISHE'S MEAL

Some months had passed since the awful night that Ed T's chunks of flesh were carried down by the wind, all the way down to the Iron Marks Cave, and the citizens of Saint Nicholas had forgotten about Ed T's mysterious killing. But I couldn't; I kept thinking about the terror that all the ethnic groups of the neighboring towns went through that ghastly night. One afternoon, I come in with my fishing tools in hand to tell Zishe that I was on my way to fishing; I took advantage at that moment and asked her tons of questions about the mysteries of the Saint Nicholas River, especially the secrets of the fishing pond and the whereabouts of the mystical secrets of Joseph, the Wizard that I had heard about. She replied to all the questions that I had asked her, and I was very happy with all her replies but wasn't able to stop thinking of Ed T's pieces of flesh diving down the cliff, reducing the chunks to ashes; my mind constantly swirled, my brain sent tragic images of the horrible crime, as I strove so hard to forget, but I couldn't think how to solve the mystery that I was trying to forget, not just yet.

That balmy day, I was in my room alone; time went by, and it turned into this gorgeous, clear, and sunny afternoon. I was deadly afraid. By now, I still didn't have the strength to set foot out the door. I went into Zishe's room, and chatted with her for a long time, in fact, I lingered with her the whole afternoon. The sun was going down so fast. By this time, I had made my mind up to stay indoors, and not go out for a week.

Suddenly, Zishe said in a deep voice, "I'm hungry, and I'm craving fish," pointing at me with her powerful Saint Nicholas Dominion scepter, known as Zishe's D rod, which the natives always refer to as ZDR; all the villagers of Sun City Territory knew that she had pulled it out of the river pond in her early thirties. It was given to her by Leerd to defend me from the deadly attacks of Joseph, the Wizard blitz. "Oh!" she reasoned, "I would give my very special blessings to the one who brings me fresh fish from the river tonight."

"Gladly!" I lowered my face and without saying a single word, trudged out the door. I chose not to withdraw until I'd grabbed her hand and kissed her goodbye. Certainly, she gave me a boost, and she charged me with supernatural strength when she pointed the ZDR at me.

I hastened to get my fishing rod and a small, old net and ran down the trail to the river. I got comfortable on my usual rock and sat on my usual stool, stretched up, and lifted my feet to rest on the two sticks rope to start my fishing quest. I attached the bait to the hook and before dropping it into the water, I made sure nobody was watching me; I was frightened because it was getting dark. It was so late, and I didn't see or hear anything. So, I felt comfortable and safe, then I went back to my fishing. I bent my elbow and stretched out my right arm to cast the line as far as I could.

There was a moment of peace and silence. Indeed, so far, all things were going well. I was doing well, and in about three minutes, I had already caught five large fish. What I had caught as yet, was more than enough. Truthfully, the catch was more than enough to feed Zishe three to five meals! But I got carried away and I wanted to try out the huge, bewitched pond, full of demon fishes, and the idea was to pull all the good fish from the tarn. Suddenly, scary noises come whispering and grew in magnitude, and moved up the water current. T was coming to get me; no doubt in my mind that he was the one who was gaslighting me, but I was sure he needed me alive.

Suddenly, a towering, skinny-man shape formed in the center of a whirlpool; it formed behind my back, standing with its feet on the ground and touching heaven with its head. That was the illusion presented to me from the reflecting image arising from the water pond. I tried to break free, but I couldn't; I didn't even have enough time to stand up. He pushed me into the deep pond, and I started sinking within a second, going fast to the pond's bottom. I saw an ugly-looking fish, the size and the shape of a shark; the hungry fish tittered at me; Joseph, the Wizard sniggered. I didn't know him till now, but I had heard tales of his devilish chuckle from the bullies at my elementary school; he was ready and rallied, trying to bite pieces of my flesh and crush my whole body to bones. A colony of colorful fish was fighting among themselves to get a bite from the hook's bait and rip off the worm that I had attached. I needed to swim up and out right away! A large, redfish swam around the hook, wrapped in a red and black flag with the words, "T's flag," written on it. It had the face of a human, the tongue and mouth of a serpent, and a fish's tail, and it had human hands and multiple feet attached from its neck to its tail.

I tried to swim up; I heard the voice of Thudil calling the strange-looking fish by its name. He ordered Zinkyoh to attack, and he said to the fish commanding and yelling, "Don't let Mike escape!"

The rare and evil fish, Zinkyoh, started to chase me. I stretched and flip-flapped my arms to swim out of its reach, but the weight of my boots I had on, were so heavy that I was not able to come up to the surface. Instead of going up, I stayed glued to the stone floor, and my feet rested on the bottom. Zinkyoh dived down showing his sharp teeth with his huge jaws wide open, and ready to crush me with a couple of bites. I was sure, I was going to be swallowed alive, and my body would be an appetizer to the human fish that was opening his jaw wide to show me his sharp and powerful iron teeth; the teeth were long, sharp, and huge! Zinkyoh was so close, to bare his curved molars at me, still opening its hungry mouth, now showing me his powerful bite by closing and opening his jaws and sticking out its long snake-like tongue. Zinkyoh lined up his body and showed his terrible teeth opening his mouth even wider to chew me up in one bite

In distress, I yelled at the top of my lungs to Leerd, saying, "HEY! FISH ME OUT!" Immediately, I saw a yellowish light ray hitting the surface of the water, the river parted in two, and opened a canal for me to stand away from the hungry fish and out of the turbulent waters; I quickly thought to go to the riverbank. But a huge net was dropped on me; it caught me and lifted me to safe ground. Once out, I dragged my feet; I wanted to get out of the net in a flash, but my strength was almost gone, and I fainted. Somehow, a current of wind blew, formed a small whirlwind, and picked up the edge of the net. I rolled my body a few times, then I came to rest on my stomach. Finally, I was out of the trap! I had the honor to watch live, the deadly brawl between Thudil and Leerd. They scuffled to get control of the river; the skirmish took place five feet away from where I was laying thinking and watching the fight. I knew that only a miracle could save my life. I also knew if Leerd took possession of the river, I had a chance to make it out alive, and go back home safe and sound to prepare Zishe's meal. I would bring the catch of the day to her for supper and get her the special blessing that she had promised me a couple of hours ago. I knew she had been talking about me with Leerd every afternoon; I wanted to know so badly what they talked about, and what mission they had planned for me. The unexpected happened in about three minutes of fighting; Leerd chased away Thudil, I got saved, and a few minutes later, I was standing still, rinsing the catch with a lot of fresh water, and washing and cleaning the small fish. I was still spitting out water from my lungs, which were still waterlogged because I had gulped even dirt when I was drowning some minutes earlier.

PROPHESY

Thirty-three minutes of throwing up algae, tadpoles, and fish poop went by; I got up with severe vertigo, and I walked wobbling and dizzy. Finally, I got back home and went straight to the kitchen to cook a delicious fish broth for Zishe. She'd been waiting for me to return, hopefully, with some fish for a tasty nosh, for she'd been craving fish for a very long time. She hadn't asked me to go fishing because she didn't want me to set foot out of the house because she was well aware that Joseph, the Wizard planned to snatch me. Soon I started to cook the soup and rustled it up in no time. I cleaned the largest fish that I had caught and fried it; I set it down on a large plate, and around it, I laid down pieces of fruit and vegetables to embellish it, and then I took it to Zishe's table. She gobbled the fish down right after she finished her goulash; she looked at the fruit and vegetables and then her heart broke, and she started to weep, as she had done for the last two years after she ate her fresh trawled fish, that I had caught myself. Not every time I had gone fishing for her, had I caught this many. Later in the afternoon, she looked up at the heavens and whispered a prayer of thanks. This afternoon, she knew that the time for me to know the true mystery of my future had come, and it must be revealed.

She told me that in a couple of years, I would become a beloved earthly superhero, and she also said, "You must know now, the details of how it's going to happen. Listen! This is according to the information I've been getting from Jud, Jed, and Jull, who are the Sons of Sun, also known as 'SOS' or the galactic wise men."

Zishe had already spent about half an hour grinding, and swallowing and chomping slowly on the big, tasty fish. I lingered with her, watching her enjoying her tasty, fishy delicatessen meal because Dr, Watters had recommended and ordered her to a strict daily fish-only diet. Patiently, I had waited for her to finish her nosh; my mind was thinking about the blessings she promised to bestow on me. All of a sudden, Zishe looked me in the eye; she'd been reading my thoughts for the last three minutes and she'd been trying to chomp a little bit faster for the last twenty-two minutes. Coughing loudly a few minutes back, she had asked me for a glass of warm water; I hesitated to give her a cup of water because she had never drunk cold water after savoring fish soup. I moved closer to her and stood in front of her; by now she had eaten up the last bite. Now, she strove to stand up, and it was clear to me that she needed a little help; I offered her a helping hand, but she refused because she needed to stand up on her own, and then she began talking. First, she begged me to rub her forehead and neck. I pummeled her neck and back gently. Second, she raised her wrinkled hands to her wrists level, and she grabbed my fishy-smelling hands to help her stand up. Third, she stood herself up on one foot, and within minutes she was dancing with me. At this point, she smiled and hummed one of her favorite songs.

Zishe moved her hands up and placed them on my head and led a brief prayer to anoint me. She ended her short but meaningful deep prayer, grabbed a hollowed piece of wood filled with light oil and poured it on my head; the sticky potion ran down my cheeks and smeared all over my neck. I raised my left hand to wipe the odorless, oily substance sliding close to my eyes.

Immediately, she stopped my hand before I touched the solution, and said, "Let it be; don't touch it, son. You need to let it sprint all over your head and over your face; it must do all the cleansing before you swab it out." Then she told me there was a prophecy about me. She also called me to kneel, then she started the swearing process, while she spoke in an unknown tongue during the anointing and swearing ceremony.

Zishe began the anointing ritual, and in a few minutes, it was all over. I was confused for all she did was soak my body in oil and pray in an unknown tongue. I stood up and asked her, "Zishe, please tell me, what's the meaning of this strange and mysterious ritual?" She dithered, then she answered me taking a long pause and staring at the window where Leerd had given her the revelation some years back.

She appraised me. "I was told a long time ago, in a special vision, that the only son of Doctor Walter Watters had been primed to become a savior, to save all the children of the world from the plot of a criminal organization of savage, and corrupt globalists, and the madness of a wicked woman to control the whole universe. In the revelation, Leerd showed me that the wicked woman intended to kill boys and girls under eighteen years of age, in a single day, and she already had evil plans of drowning all the children of the world in a single night, on a hidden beach in the Pacific Ocean." Leerd also informed her that this organization of criminals was already working around the clock in a hole-and-corner laboratory in Silicon Valley, developing a formula to make medicine for all adult humans to live eternally and to have only same-sex marriages to halt procreation. Zishe paused for a few seconds. I stretched out my legs and looked out the window where Zishe had been fixing her eyes a minute ago. She moved her lips fast as if she was having a face-to-face conversation with somebody standing by the window. I was scared and focused hard to read her lips.

Zishe ended her conversation with the invisible being and turned toward me. She said, "This is what I was told that frightening night when Leerd defeated Thudil for the first fearful battle I saw between good and evil. The promise was that within five years, the SOS men will visit you, and they'll discuss a heavenly matter that had been given to them by Jus Supp, the Lord, and Creator of the universe, and Maker of the mysteries and the riddles around his holy making. Jus Supp, the one who guides and leads his supernatural, divine creation of day and night, twenty-four-seven, three hundred and sixty-five days a year, is the beginning, and he will guide it all with no end. Then, I saw the three Sons of Sun: Jud, Jed, and Jull coming down from the innermost circle of the sun; it was the day you were born. They came down quickly and energetically to tell me that you'll be vested and empowered with a superpowered yellow and silver suit. They notified me that your name was going to be 'MegAm,' which is ordered by a decree signed by Jus Supp that you'll be called Mega-Superhero man."

I started shivering and shaking; I twisted my tongue, and my words came out in a different and unknown dialect. I was talking with Zishe in an unfamiliar language; she knew that the prophecy was going to come true shortly. She took a last quick look out the window; I followed her with my eyes wide open. A single lightning ray flashed in the sky and swooped beneath the brisk breeze; the tip of it stopped at the window and started to write a line in golden letters. I covered my eyes for a second because I was frightened. I dared to look at the unknown object again, which was still writing and carving the special marks on the wooden window. Zishe marched towards the window.

I yelled, "Watch out Zishe; please don't get too close!" But before I could warn her, she was already placing the palm of her hand on the inscription. Leerd retrieved her fingertips and allowed her to place them on the flaring characters. She stared at the burning marks for a few seconds and walked back to her rocking chair. I just looked on, but I didn't dare to ask her questions.

Gaily, she hummed, "Mission is completed today, son, and your task and challenges are about to begin!"

REIGO'S LASSO

Two weeks passed, and this morning, I woke up early, picked up my fishing rod at sunrise, and hurried to catch fresh fish for Zishe. It was a five-minute walk to the JW Iron Lair Pond, a shore off Saint Nicholas' brook. I hopped through glades of towering pine trees. Suddenly, I saw a huge Coral snake that was blocking my path; the poisonous reptile was ready to attack me; her head was elevated, and she was sticking her tongue in and out to show her deadly fangs. I couldn't go around because every direction was blocked, so, jumping over the snake was the only way, and the only road to get to the riverbank. I needed to come up with a plan of action right away. But I was glad that I had seen the colorful viper in time before the snake went for a bite at my heel. When the snake tried my heels, I jumped out of her reach in time, and I sprinted to escape in a hurry. Finally, the Coral snake gave up the chase and I made it to the stream; I was still in panic mode. I didn't waste any time, because I was in a hurry to make it back home to serve breakfast to Zishe. I dropped the line and the hook deep into the water. All of a sudden, I heard a strange noise in the distance. I looked around, but I saw nothing out of the ordinary and I kept my eyes on the line to watch closely for a vibration. Nevertheless, the whistling came closer every second. I froze and felt goosebumps. I started to think about danger and became stressed; I raised my arms to pour out all the water from the fishing bucket. I was certain I needed to dart away quickly. But it was a little too late; I heard the sound of hooves; a horse was dashing and galloping toward me, but the funny thing was I didn't see anything or anybody around. I got ready to put away my fishing tools.

I looked to the left riverbank, and I saw a huge shadow of a man riding a big horse, reflecting in the water; it was a white horse scurrying close behind me, and the rider was getting ready to charge at me. With his lasso in hand, he swung the rope a few times to throw the loop over me. I was trapped, for the turbulent water was in front of me, and the beast and the rider were pouncing from the rear end. I saw the loop opening and flying over my head, with the loop opening in the air forming a circle and dropping over my neck. I felt it going over my head, scratching my ears, and landing at the scruff of my neck. I moved my right hand to grasp the loop, and I just had enough time to put my fingers in the loop before it could tighten around my throat and choke me to death. The cowboy sped his horse away to tighten the loop, and drag me to my death; luckily, I protected my neck with my fingers. I was dragged around the river shore for about two hundred yards. Reigo untied the lasso from the saddle pommel, and he got off the horse and came to stand next to me to mock me and spit in my face. He thought I was already dead; I played dead, but my neck was only bruised, my fingers' flesh were severely torn to the bone, and I suffered slashes and bruises all over my body. Blood was coming out of my ears, mouth, and eyes, my throat was covered in bruises and cuts, and blood was running down my throat. The demon rider guffawed and yelled to his horse to turn around, and he started dragging and torturing my body for a second lap. He hauled my body up the stream and turned around; he slowed the pace of his horse and came to a sudden stop for a second. After he untied the lasso from the pommel, he got off and came to me. He turned me on my back and spat in my face a second time. He uncovered his face for me to see, but I couldn't see his face for I was seeing double, and my vision was blurry and I didn't recognize him.

He aimed the barrel of his rifle at my head, but he didn't pull the trigger. He said, "You are already as good as dead, not worthy to spend a shot to blow your brain out when you're already done!" He continued, "I am Joseph, the Wizard, and Dumb-Dumb Thudil's right-hand man here on earth. Mission accomplished; the vultures will eat you on my call even if you are still alive."

I faked being dead; I knew my hand had saved me from choking, and after Reigo left, somehow, I managed to get free and stand up. I picked up the only fish I had caught and headed back home. Zishe saw me when I was coming, and she literally yanked me by my hair to bring me inside from the front yard where I had fainted a minute ago. She prayed for me, and Dr. Watters took care of my bruised and wounded body. In about two weeks, I was completely healed, and I went back to the Iron Lair Pond, fishing for Zishe once again.

JOSEPH, THE WIZARD'S ARSENAL

Three months after Reigo had beaten me up, I started getting revelations and visions. One morning, at the top of the midnight hour, Joseph, the Wizard left the conference room; he had been putting together plans to kidnap me with Thudil and a bunch of high-ranking demons in the inky shadow-floating castle. He was escorted by the twelve high-security demons and brought out of the "Demons' Iron Mark."

Meanwhile, I was snoring in bed and had no idea that my life was going to be hell for the rest of my days, and that I needed to fight back to survive the multiple attacks from Joseph, the Wizard which was going to be unleashed upon me. It was six in the morning; I jumped to my feet, grabbed my fishing equipment, and I plonked my hat on because I was going to stay late, taking care of the old skinny caw we owned. I had to feed the animal along the river shore so she could munch fresh grass once a week. Zishe quaffed her vitamin C every day, from fresh milk from the spotted scraggly old cow. A few minutes later, I was walking through thorn hedges along the dirt trail, and I was singing one of the original songs that I was writing, my guitar hanging on my right shoulder. A cantina, full of fresh drinking water, was secured to my sash. I carried the fishing rod in my right hand and a short, dirty hawser in my left hand. The bovine knew her way very well and ran ahead of me to drink water, and to munch all the green grass she needed to fill her tum.

I got a message through a personal and real vision: a bright lightning ray came down from heaven and landed in front of me; I stopped. Another ray followed and hit the ground behind me; a third ray descended and fell to my right side, and the last one delved a hole to my left. I was watching the whole time, but the good thing was, I wasn't scared at all, and a very powerful positive energy filled my mind. I was capsuled for a few minutes inside four thick transparent and fluorescent light walls; the crystal walls touched heaven and went deep into the ground. I read a red-green-blue inscription on the wall that encouraged me to get on my knees and pray. I did engage my thoughts to talk for a long time to the Maker of all things, Jus Supp. A second after I finished my meditation, the walls were moved up to heaven; the one in front was lifted by a white crystal-clear hand, the one on my back went up a second later, and the ones on my sides were lifted at the same time. My body was as bright as the sun, and my heart was full of endless joy. Immediately, I started fishing; it was getting hot and the sun's rays were hitting the surface of the water like magnets in the water. I must say, that it was a clear day and in a few minutes, I caught three big fish. I thought that I was going to catch enough fish to feed Zishe for the whole month. But trouble was about to spoil my day. A bullet missed me by a hair, and a second one burned the hair on the top of my head.

Joseph, the Wizard was behind me; he spoke rough and tough, "Don't dare to move!" he said. I turned very slowly to take a look at the wicked killer, who had a deadly .44 Magnum in his right hand, and a Smith & Wesson XVR 460, an extreme velocity revolver, in his left hand. A large-caliber assault rifle was fastened across his chest. Two leather ammunition cartridge belts were strapped to his right shoulder, underneath his rifle. A pure leather holster was clipped to his belt, with a .22 short mini revolver sheathed in it. He had seven hand grenades hanging on his legs, two hand-made cloth belts tied to his upper legs, countless knives, daggers, and a machete decorated the mutilation scars all over his body. He wore a green uniform painted with skeletons, and sculls painted with horns. Oh, boy! He was a monster, and his face was tattooed with demons. His fingernails were about three inches long. Indeed, he was the son of Lucifer, walking in human form.

As he was leaving, he told me, "I was hired to kill you, but not today. First I was told to gaslight you; I want to have some fun torturing you. I'll be watching you every day! I promise you; you'll die a painless death. Today was a way to introduce myself and to get to know you better." I was sure I had made top-notch enemies since Zishe anointed me for my future mission.

I was aware that if I followed the instructions Zishe and Leerd had given me a short time ago, in the four pillars of the light walls, I would win any battle. I packed all my equipment and tied the rope around the cow's horns to lead her back home to take Zishe the fish on time, for she survived only on fish and milk; it was her mandatory diet every day to please

Leerd and for blessings from the Lord of creation, the Great Lord Jus Supp, to her and me.

Many days went by, and I hadn't seen the Beast (the nickname I gave Joseph, the Wizard) for the last three weeks. I was having fun playing my guitar, fishing, and daydreaming of becoming the greatest guitar player and the best singer-songwriter the world had ever known. In fact, I had forgotten about the Beast's threat, and I thought I wasn't going to see or deal with his scary, scarred face anymore.

I went back to my normal, peaceful life, and I went to the Lair Pond every afternoon to catch fresh fish for Zishe. It never came to my mind that Joseph, the Wizard was putting together an ingenious plan to torment, and gaslight me first, and then finish me off with a spear of fire going through my heart, as a sacrifice to please his evil master, Thudil. He was working behind closed doors; these were the orders he passed down to his wicked demons to torment me bit by bit, but I knew Leerd the light supplier was doing battle to keep me safe. Thudil, the fallen demon chief, had already been warned that Leerd would protect me to anoint me as a superhero.

ALMOST DIVINE

Joseph, the Wizard retired for a while; he stopped raiding and gaslighting me. After twenty-five days of fun and good times fishing, I became used to enjoying my life, and no fretting came into my head, but not for long, because my luck was about to change, I was having a good time, and I was very happy, and I expected that my future life would be full of joy too. In my thoughts, it was absolutely zilch, since I was sure I would be relaxing and enjoying my time, for the rest of my life.

It was a clear afternoon, and just a minute before, I had had a quick chat with Zishe. I had watched every single movement she made, and by now I was used to reading her body language. Suddenly, I stared at her; she looked tired, and slowly she raised her divine ZDR and pointed to the window. A single lightning ray came down, zigzagging, and hit the window with a golden arrow carving and writing, and a long hand holding the pointed shank. Surely, it was a sign for me to go fishing at the turbulent Lair Pond. Immediately, I grabbed my armor and went out the front door. I was singing acapella, but all of a sudden, I saw a dead body laying across the narrow trail. It blocked my path; I jumped to step over the cadaver. I strode around making my way through thick grass and thorn bushes, but I was walking in a circle looking at the dead body. I heard a moan and a weak voice calling for help; I saw the back of the human body. Curiously, it was dressed in Joseph's strange uniform, and I jumped over from one side to the other to see his face which was buried in the mud. I was in shock watching the horrible scene; indeed, it was the Wizard dying; his head had been smashed and stuck to the dusty and muddy ground and had turned into an elongated pancake covered with his blood, instead of maple syrup, and a huge rock was on top of his head. I was sure, he was already dead; a voice called me from the distance, pleading with me to roll the stone from his head. I hesitated to move my body in any direction, as my feet were glued to the rocky terrain. I wanted to take a step back, but a force moved me forward. My right foot slid a couple of feet; I tried to slide it back, but my left foot was already sliding level with my right one. Soon, I was rolling the stone with the tip of my right index finger. I was mesmerized that the rock moved just with a little push of my index finger!

Instantly, Joseph, the Wizard's face, was healing and in a matter of seconds, it was reconstructed! Truly, it was a miracle that the Beast was showing before my own eyes. And I saw an angel flying down and landing next to him; he was picking his body up and putting him back on his feet.

The angel flew back up in the sky, and Joseph spoke loudly and clearly, "I was almost dead but I'm a demon," he paused a bit, "I meant, you just saw Michael, the Archangel, my best friend and partner for life, that came to pay me an urgent visit." Joseph, the Wizard added, "He always saved me when I was in trouble." Joseph made it clear that, as a matter of fact, I haven't forgotten about you pal, but I've been busy running some important errands for Thudil." He slapped my left cheek and released a second blow to my right cheek, but I ducked in time; then he said, "Today, I have enough free time to spare and to have some fun with you; I tell you, I contrived some out-of-this-world tricks, and I want to spend quality time showing them to you. Don't you think it's a good idea?" he asked with a thunderous and roaring voice that echoed as it hit every mountain and hill nearby. Immediately, a dozen short, fat soldiers came and formed a circular, tall wall around us. I spun around twice to find a gap to break free and fled. I ran and pushed the shortest soldier; I thought that he was going to fall when I charged him, but he was pinned to the ground and he didn't move a hair, and I thought he would fly a mile!

I just surrendered and buried my face in my hands. I fell in the dust and started to pray, and I asked Leerd for protection and to rescue me. Then, Jus Supp heard me and sent his son, Leerd to fight for me. I saw Joseph, the Wizard drawing his guns and firing at Leerd. Joseph, the Wizard kept hurling all his weapons, but he was losing the battle, in fact, all his soldiers were already dead on the ground. He grabbed his rifle, knelt on one knee, and aimed to fire a second round at the target, which was me and firing at close range. I watched, then I touched my whole body to make sure I hadn't been pierced with lead, and I wanted to count how many holes I had in my body. Leerd had covered me with an invisible wall of fire to protect me, just seconds before Joseph, the Wizard started launching at me, but the screen dome stopped every bullet that had been shot at me.

Joseph, the Wizard loaded his rifle with another round of ammunition, and he repeated the loading over and over again until he ran out of ammunition. He looked around and saw all his men dead; he knew he had been defeated. He ran around the thick jungle and then fled. Surely, I had been saved a second time from Joseph, the Wizard's deadly ambush, in the nick of time.

My destiny was to survive, and in time, become a superhero, according to Zishe's prophesy. Jud, Jed, and Jull, the sunny bros, would be on a mission, and walking around planet earth looking for me to anoint and change my name to MegAm, according to Zishe's omen. Because Leerd had assured her that nobody was going to stop the prophecy from coming true.

DR. WATTERS' JAUNT

Joseph, the Wizard, walked around the Lair Pond, five minutes before midnight. He spent his time loading his rifle and cleaning his favorite knife. Then he stepped in the middle of the Demons Ingress Iron Mark; this entering mark is also known as FERRI D DIABLO to the local aborigines, who fish along the riverbank for fifty miles. Suddenly, a water whirlwind formed in the middle of the pond. With the speed of light, it built an arch, elevated about 500 feet into the sky, and bent, forming a water arch going down in the form of a water tunnel. It stretched its tip to reach the Demons Ingress Iron Mark entrance, where Joseph, the Wizard was waiting to be lifted. He turned to the bridge and stared for a couple of minutes. Immediately, the bridge froze, and it became a solid ice bridge. Joseph, the Wizard was marked on the forehead by one of the twelve demons that were escorting him. He walked over the bridge and entered a tiny hole; he was sucked into a funnel and submerged into the water to enter Thudil's Castle. He returned three minutes later with a note in hand. Joseph, the Wizard exited the ice bridge and stopped to read the devilish message. The order had been given to gaslight Dr. Watters. The ice bridge melted and showered over the pond. Joseph, the Wizard hailed Thudil as he was walking, and screamed his way out, he was ready to play mind games with Dr. Watters, that was for sure!

Meanwhile, at about two in the morning, the same night, I couldn't sleep at all because I had a dreadful migraine. I saw the lights at Dr. Watters' lab flickered on; I took a peek to make sure he was as fine. Indeed, he was; he was checking his medical supplies and doing his yearly inventory.

Dr. Watters found out that he was running out of medical supplies, and he needed to take an emergency trip to Sun City to buy more medicine; his faithful friend was helping him with the inventory. Finally, they finished the counting, and Dr. Watters was escorted by his trustworthy friend and servant, John Rudelir. John saddled three horses on Dr. Watters' request; they took two horses to ride on, and a third one to carry the loads back from the city. The journey was nineteen miles one way and about a forty-three miles round trip. They left at three in the morning because they had to return the same day. They didn't have any other option. Dr. Watters planned it that way; the plan was, they were going to do the shopping quickly, but Dr. Watters worried that they had to visit three pharmaceutical providers to find the best deals and look for promotions to save some money. The drug stores were spread about a mile apart.

Eventually, they arrived at the first location; the town cathedral's old clock showed 9:33 AM. They were a bit early and waited several minutes for the store to open at 10:00 sharp. Around 12:09 P.M. they made it to the second one, which was packed with villagers and burghers looking for the best deals, and it took Dr. Watters a long time just to place his lengthy order. After two hours, they loaded two big wooden boxes, made with rough and ready logs, and tied them with ropes to the horse's back.

Nearly forty-five minutes later, they were riding to the last location, and in a matter of minutes, Dr. Watters snapped up a few items that he still needed, wrapped the medical supplies as fast as they could, then strolled in at a nearby fancy restaurant to eat a late lunch for they were starving. John Rudelir made sure to give the horses a lot of water, and enough food, and groomed them to prepare them for the long ride back to Saint Nicholas Village.

At five in the afternoon, Dr. Watters and John Rudelir had reached the city limit; they took a last quick look back at the tall buildings. The sun was still shining but moving fast to take cover in the west. Because they had a long trip ahead of them and it was already late, they scooted the horses forward. According to Dr. Watters' reckoning, the estimated time to get back home was roughly six hours. They had to keep hustling before the sun set, to avoid confrontations with robbers from many of the most violent villages that they had to go through. After three hours of nonstop galloping, the horses were tired, and dragging their hooves; they needed to rest the animals. Dr. Watters decided to go forward forty-five more minutes to climb up to the top of the mountain and make it to the peak before taking a breather. They stopped at the plateau and took a long break.

They had already climbed 3,000 feet; they trekked up, and they were already halfway to their final destination.

The rest of the way was only a drop ride to Saint Nicholas Village. John Rudelir found a good spot to rest, lay down on his back, first grabbed a long rock, put it under his head, and then closed his eyes. Meanwhile, Dr. Watters kept guard and took several steps north to watch the dim lights at Sun City. A minute later he moved west to enjoy the view of the majestic coastal flatlands in the Pacific Ocean. Next, he walked south to look down from a distance at his beloved Saint Nicholas Village; he was hoping to spot the awesome Saint Nicholas River running its waters west through the fertile farming fields that majestically watered the trees, fruits, and vegetables to provide food for the people. Lastly, he went clockwise to end east, and he stared for a long time, enjoying the view of the high peaks of the treeless Sierra Madre Mountain.

At 9:00 PM, the horses were galloping next to each other, going down the hill again, but rested and well-fed. Dr. Watters and his companion, John Rudelir descended more than a mile while engaging in a long conversation, Suddenly, Dr. Watters stopped, and the four-legged, gentle animal refused to proceed. Dr. Watters whipped his horse a couple of times to go forward, but out of the corner of his eye, Dr. Watters saw a rider on the back of a mean-looking horse. The horse rider was wearing a black mask and hood and was dressed in a green military uniform, with a shining double-edged sword in hand. Dr. Watters' horse jumped, then halted, and Dr. Watters fell off; he got up as fast as he could, dusted off his clothes, and got back on the horse's back. He looked around, but the horse rider was gone. He looked around again, but the masked man was nowhere to be seen.

John Rudelir noticed and asked Dr. Watters, "Are you OK?" Dr. Watters just nodded. John Rudelir asked again, "What happened, Dr. Watters?"

He replied in a soft, broken voice, "I fell asleep for a second, and I fell off my horse, that's all." Of course, Dr. Watters was lying because he didn't want to scare his faithful, trustworthy friend. Dr. Watters really cared for his beloved servant and didn't want him to be afraid the rest of the way.

At 11:00 PM, they entered the City of Juphyll which was located a mile from Saint Nicholas' huge green valley. Dr. Watters noticed that they'd been followed. He turned his head back and saw the horse almost tailgating them. He sprinted the horses to get rid of the mysterious evil spirit; he took shortcuts and detours, but so did the unknown horseback rider following him. The masked rider kept following them from the entrance to the exit of Juphyll town, hiding in the semi-dark streets and disappearing in the shadows. The curs' barking faded away. Dr. Watters and his companion kept a steady pace. He hoped to make it to the crossroads, safe and sound. But somehow, the mysterious rider had passed them, and he was already blocking the crossroads.

The rider was waiting for them in the middle of the three ways crossroads; he was swinging his unsheathed sword to block their way. To the right, the strange rider pointed Dr. Watters to go and moved sideways to obstruct the straight road, which was the one they needed to take. Dr. Watters had the option to go. Going to the left was a mistake, certainly choosing suicide because it went to a dead-end trail that led to the town's cemetery. A huge lightning beam came down from the dark, foggy sky, and focused for about thirty-three seconds on the wicked rider's eyes, blinding him temporarily. John Rudelir hurried his horse to a stampede when he saw that it was Joseph, the Wizard blocking the road. Joseph, the Wizard moved his horse to the left and Dr. Watters took the chance to go through the other side. They both managed to pass by and flee. Instantly, they spurred their horses to gallop even faster for three-quarters of a mile without even turning their heads to look back. The horses were tired, sweaty, and thirsty. They arrived at a small, almost dry brook, called Yuphyll Gutter; it was exactly midnight. The horses lowered their long necks to quench their thirst at the small water-mixed-with-mud ponds.

A scary voice came from the other side of the narrow, sharp, rocky brook, calling Dr. Watters, "I am introducing myself," the voice sounded, "My name is Joseph, the Wizard, and I work for Thudil, the lord of the forces of darkness. I was hired to kill your son, Mike Watters. This is a warning!" the voice ended. Dr. Watters' mind went back, way back to when he was a lad himself, to retrieve information given to him by his father. It took him a couple of seconds to remember one scary night, he had been riding with his dad; he heard an unholy racket and demonic roars, and Lucifer had grabbed the reins of his dad's horse and tried to pull him down by snatching and grabbing his left leg. He heard the words of his Pops, *"In Jus Supp, I trust, only him I serve and follow. Get away from me, Satan, in the name of my Lord, I chide you!"* Dr. Watters recited the same phase his dad had used so long ago.

John Rudelir was as cold as ice, pinning his butt to the horse's saddle. A strong wind started up between them and blew Joseph, the Wizard away momentarily to oblivion. About nineteen minutes later, they were unharmed, opening the gate to Dr, Watters' home. John Rudelir refused to listen to Dr. Watters' warning to sleep in his house and went back to his own place. Dr. Watters couldn't sleep the rest of the night, thinking about the fellow he had met at the brook, and the threats he made toward his son, Mike.

THE CROSS ON CHILLS

A neighborly, human shadow stood in the middle of a gigantic, mystical office at Satan's castle; demonic roars were reverberating through the cloud of fog. Joseph, the Wizard's roar was carried by air around the pond. He was talking about the evil strategy to gaslight Dr. Watters that night, all the way from Bastille to Saint Nicholas Village on the way back. Thudil spoke, and Joseph, the Wizard just listened to his master for a few minutes. Then, a big penstock fell on him, and like a funnel, sucked him and the twelve demons up, and took them to the Demon Ingress Iron *Mark*.

Later, at 10:11 PM, Dr. Watters was called out on an emergency doctor's visit. He needed to go to the Bastille Hills village, which was located a mile away from Saint Nicholas. A strange man used to walk up and down the hill on a narrow, sharp, and stony road every night, to secure and protect the road from Joseph, the Wizard's strikes, and he chased away bad spirits. He made sure to do it every single night, from dusk to dawn. He left his hut at 6 PM and came back home at 6:00 each morning. The interesting thing was that he never tripped or fell in the dark; he carried a long, wooden cross on his shoulders and dragged it the whole trip.

He was dressed in unique attire: he covered his head with a dirty hand-made rope crown tied with an old piece of worn cloth, and he carried more than a dozen old, smudged kitchen utensils, including pots, pans, buckets, and a set of pewter dishes. Neighboring towns' people thought he came from a Bedouin tribe in the Middle East. Indeed, he was a riveting, scary-looking man, but he was sweet, gentle, and harmless; his real name was Daniel Gabriel, but neighbors had chosen the nickname, Chills, based on his appearance and the only word he ever spoke was chill, chill, chill. Neighbors had never heard him say any other word.

It was one night, around 5:55 PM, when a rich farmer came to Dr. Watters' property; he tied his white-yellowish horse, called Dimond, to a barbed wire fence. He took a quick look at the sun dimming its light, then he walked head down to the lab to ask Dr. Watters for an emergency call to his house, because his only son, Edgar Salt, was dying from an extremely high fever and high blood pressure. Half an hour later, Dr. Watters and the farmer stood next to Edgar's bed, and after a quick evaluation, Dr. Watters came up with a strange diagnosis and told the farmer that Edgar had been stung by an unknown poisonous insect.

He gave him a shot of stinky, red antidote, and he applied an antibacterial cream to the infected area, after he had cleaned the wound with alcohol, and massaged the swollen lump to reduce the pain of the inflammation. All of a sudden, Dr. Watters started to hear strange voices piercing the walls. The farmer encouraged the doctor not to pay attention to the noises because they were friendly moans of Chill's close, and invisible spiritual friends waiting for him and speaking in tongues. When Chills first came to stay in his house, the farmer had built a nice shack on his own lot for Chills, and that was twenty-three years ago, when Chills first arrived from an unknown place, begging for food and a place to live. Before leaving, Dr. Watters warned the farmer that his son, Edgar, would die within twenty-eight hours. Dr. Watters left thirteen minutes before midnight, not knowing the danger he was to face on the rocky, dirt road up the hill. He had to climb the dark and narrow path for fifteen minutes to get to the top of the hill. He had ridden his horse halfway up the hill when the trouble started.

He was having a bad time because he kept thinking about Edgar's lethal poison. Suddenly, the horse stopped and refused to go forward; he whipped the horse to make the animal go ahead. Dr. Watters' skin got goosebumps, demoniac voices and laughter invaded his ears, and he became weak and scared. He pinned his butt to the saddle and squeezed the reins tightly. He pushed the horse to go ahead, but the force of darkness was coming like a tornado to sweep both him and the horse away to hellfire; he thought of a prayer for a second. He recited his usual prayer, hoping to chase away the tormenting voices from his ears, but not a chance, the demons roared and whistled even closer to his ears. A human body fell from the sky and out of nowhere, landed on the back of the horse. He grabbed Dr. Watters' waist and squeezed his stomach. The horse felt the heavy load and galloped up the rest of the way. Dr. Watters never gave up on his prayer the rest of the way.

The horse was tired and almost fell, before they got to the top of the mountain where Dr. Watters expected and hoped to ask for some help. He went inside the first abandoned hut located several yards from the top of the hill. He moaned out as loud as he could, but no one answered him. Surely, in the mind of Dr. Watters, he was already in the hands of Joseph, the Wizard, who was riding on the back of his horse. There was no way to escape, and he was going to be devoured alive by Satan. Evidently, Jus Leerd was called for help, and he sent his messenger, Chills, who was near, pulling the cross; he went out of his way to save the dying horse and Dr. Watters. Chills was dragging his cross faster on the way back to his home from his midnight round. He sounded a hand-made shofar; Chills had blown the goat's horn three times.

Joseph, the Wizard heard the horn sounding loud, and he was in a panic; he jumped off the horse in a second and ran away. The voice of Joseph, the Wizard swearing and cursing Chills, the guardian of evil, was fading away within seconds. The horse got back its energy and moved fast up the hill. Dr. Watters got back his strength and his spirit rejoiced. A few yards ahead, he saw a shadow slowly moving down the narrow road. Dr. Watters pulled the reins to stop the horse for there was no room to let the shadowy man pass by; the figure came closer, and he was at a distance that Dr. Watters saw that it was Chills lugging his cross. Now Dr. Watters found out what the mission of the ragged man and his cross was. He guarded the road at night and certainly had saved his precious life this night. He lugged his cross and looked at Dr. Watters, who moved his horse to the right to give him some room to walk through. Dr. Watters waved him goodbye.

The knight-in-shining-armor, the hero of Bastille, armed with a cross, stopped and turned his head and gave Dr, Watters a gentle smile; he kept Dr. Watters' hopes to live, alive, and he said, "Chill, chill, chill," three times in a low and slow voice. Dr. Watters found out this same night, where Chill's name came from and that the rumors were true.

ZISHE'S WEEPING

I had been working long hours, writing and arranging a song, titled Ann Angel, but one of the chord progressions was giving me a hard time. I was livid, and tossed the pen against the wall, creased the paper I was writing on, couldn't hide my anger, and riffed a note many times, violently, and I busted a couple of strings, breaking them on purpose.

Six minutes later, I went to Zishe's room; to my surprise, she was swimming in a pool of tears. She'd been mewling like a baby and grieving painfully. I asked her, "Zishe, is everything alright?"

Amazingly, she said loudly and clearly, "C." I thought she had told me yes in Spanish, which spells (Si) for yes because it has the same sound as the letter C.

I hesitated and answered her, "Si, Gramma, I'm going fishing in an hour. I'll be back with plenty of fresh fish." I rushed out the door, turned around and stopped for a second, and said, "I promise!"

Zishe smiled and told me, "Hold it. I'm not talking about fish but the missing chord you're looking for, for your new song's chord progression. I'm sure the chord C will work perfectly for the chord progression you are trying to find."

I asked her in shock, "How do you know about the new song I'm working on?" She just nodded and kissed me; I went out yelling, enlivened by the event. I said as I was walking slowly, "Thank you, Zishe, for all the help and support," and said, "I love you." A few minutes later, on the way to the riverbank and moving slowly, I kept humming the chords together, and I noticed that they fit as perfectly as a key fits in a keyhole. Twenty minutes later, I had already trawled three medium fish. But an unexpected event was about to pop wide open. I turned my head to the right to stare up the river. The current was swaying as a colony of colorful fish stood on their tails going downstream, and I watched the water current majestically dancing when the strong updrafts of wind began rotating, and the water was filled to overflowing with enchanted golden snakes moving fast, twisting, and curving down the hills, diving and swimming up the river current. I saw a strange man coming at a distance, but I could not tell who was walking to meet me, because he was still far away. Although I was sure he was looking for me, I was frightened because I didn't know who he was or what he wanted from me. In no time, he stood behind me; I wondered how he got there so fast.

He started to speak to me, and he spoke to me sweetly and gently; his words were powerful, true, and convincing. It took twenty minutes for the weird guy to brainwash me into going with him to the Daredevils Dam to watch him doing his unique and deadly diving ploys. Zishe had warned me many times to stay away from that demonic dam, built across the Saint Nicholas River. I was shaking just at the thought that I had disobeyed her, and I didn't realize that my life was now on the line. Dr. Watters had also warned me not to talk to or trust strangers. I had no idea why I let Rudy Eagle trick me and take me to the mysterious bewitched dam.

He started to climb to the top of the tallest pine tree, planted on the highest hill around the dam; the tree was standing alone next to the huge swimming pool the dam forged. For the first time in my life, I was watching an amazing live show prepared especially for me. I turned my head around, and my eyes down to the crystal-clear water to watch the colorful fish swimming and jumping three feet high. The fish looked weird; some of them had three heads, and others had no heads at all; then I turned back up to the spot where Rudy Eagle was standing; he was watching me and waving at me to keep my eyes on him for he was ready to perform just for me. Truthfully, it was a show that I would never see again in my life. He waved at me a second time and pointed his index finger and his middle one at his eyes as a signal for me to pay close attention and follow his jump.

He yelled, "Keep your eyes wide open, my main man!" Slowly, he leaned his body forward and jumped up high, then he turned his neck to the sides, almost at the same time he moved his head forward and backward while he was jumping up. He arched his body backward and pulled it back forward while he was suspending his body in the air for a couple of seconds, as he had turned his arms into wings to flutter in the air. A bizarre and mystical transformation happened to his head: his nose and his mouth turned into the extremely sharp and curved beak of an eagle, and his head into a bird's head! Every movement he made was perfect, and he did it in slow motion. He performed especially for me to watch the whole show; it seemed, he didn't want me to turn my eyes away, not even for a split second while he was whooping, as he was going to plunge into the dam.

Indeed, he didn't want me to miss any second of his fall; he wanted me to know the real reason why he was nicknamed Rudy the Eagleman. Finally, he stretched out his arms and they converted into two airplane-like wings. He dove, and he landed, splashing, and he did not sink into the water. He wanted and expected me to see his body not sink when he hit the water. Something out of this world happened; he opened his hands and stretched his large, hooked claws, and his talons grew large as werewolves', his fingers, and his chest started to grow eagle feathers, his stomach transformed into a duck's body, and he grew feathers on his whole body; a couple of seconds after he landed on the water, he slid on top of the water without making a single splash.

Back at Dr. Watters' home, Zishe was staring out the window, just to check the time by looking at the sun's position in the sky. She realized that it was getting late; she knew I should have been back at least an hour ago. She showed signs of fatigue, and she was worried, and very hungry, almost starving for she'd been waiting for her fish to eat it for supper. She burst into non-stop weeping, and tears flowed from her eyes. And all she did was hope that I made it back home soon, safe and sound. and she prayed that Jus Supp would keep me alive. Also, she requested him to protect me, sending his son, Leerd to lead me home.

But, at the dam, I was watching the last swooping performance shown especially for my enjoyment and entertainment. Ruddy Eagle did a perfect jump and plunged into the lake, this time sinking into the water.

I clapped in admiration. I was not aware that a second later, Rudy would attack me; he would place his eagle hooked, dirty, and bloody paws on my throat, almost breaking my skin, to cut my throat. I turned west to watch the sun setting and then turned back to escape from Rudy, who was still hiding under the water, getting ready to strike. I knew that I had to be running back home for my life and waited for a chance to flee. But in a second, Rudy was already facing me and blocking the only road I could take to run far away from his knives, but he quickly reached my neck to wrap his claws around it, to cut my head off with his long, sharp eagle feet. Finally, it was time for Rudy, himself, to show up; he transformed back into an eagle man, with the head of a man, but he still had the long, curved bill of a hawk, winged arms, and the legs of a royal man standing in front of me. The bird was ready to lift me and take me to the tallest cliff to cut off my neck and roll it down the mountain and drop my dead, headless body into the cornfields, descending some thirty-three thousand feet. In the end, my body was going to be food for wild dogs and vultures.

Now, I learned for the first time, why Rudy was known in town as Rudy. Eagle-man. I just closed my eyes in defeat and yelled out the name of Zishe; the echo was carried throughout all villages in the huge valley. People started to spread the rumor that Ed Tower's killer was on the loose again and had attacked and killed another human. They just needed to wait for the next day to find out who Lucifer had caught this time. But this day, luck was on my side; the bird turned completely back into his human form. I saw Rudy in front of me, turning from a killer eagle to a wild man with a killing drive in his eyes and a sharp, shining blade in his right hand. It was a double-edged knife touching the Adam's apple of my throat, and he was ready to slide the cold iron to cut off my head. Suddenly, he pulled it away with a very slow movement and a slight, gentle smile.

He said in a mean voice, "Joseph, the Wizard hired me to kill you, but Dr. Watters, your Pops, has been kind to me, and my whole family, and for this reason, I'm not going to hurt you," He added, "Go, run fast to your house, and don't dare to look back! I don't want you to see what I'm going to do till you get back home, safely!"

I ran and pushed my tired legs to get extra speed; I reached the place where I had been fishing, within five minutes. I made a quick stop to pick up my fishing rod and the fish that I had caught earlier and ran straight home. My heart beat so fast and kept pounding in my chest, and my brain worked diligently to keep me on the alert to watch out and move forward, but my body needed the stamina to finish the final three hundred yards to reach the entrance to the gate, to go into the garden. Finally, I went inside the front door and entered Zishe's room. I came in to console her for she had been weeping again for a long time, worried about me, so I wiped her tears with the palm of my hands.

JOSEPH, THE WIZARD'S SIEGE

Joseph, the Wizard, planned his evil plot with the help of Matilda Watters, Dr' Watters' close relative. She was twenty-three years old, skinny, and single, she was also a crossed-eyed girl. She was raped and kidnapped by Joseph, the Wizard when she was fourteen years old.

That awful night, I remember, his armed men were standing around Dr. Watters' house for an undetermined amount of time, to kidnap me. Doctor Watters secured the doors; he went inside a hut to get a couple of rifles and three guns that General Constantine had left on the table, then returned to lock all the windows, locking his family in and blocking easy access to the army, led by Commander Abel Kaine, who Joseph, the Wizard had chosen to carry out his attack, and to complete the kidnapping mission. Thudil had released a bunch of spiders to set a web net to catch me. Time went by slowly, and the house had been under siege for the previous three days. Zishe hadn't been able to eat her mandated amount of fish to survive. I didn't go out fishing a single time, and Dr. Watters' patients were dying in their houses for they had already run out of medication by now.

One of his patients took a trip to visit Dr. Watters and found out that the madman had an army of demons and soldiers around the walls, and they were already clambering up the walls and bringing gimlets to bore holes in the concrete roof, for it to plummet inside the building, to get me. The patient ran back and gathered all the nearby residents to fight and save us. All of them came to free us, or at least, that was their goal, but in a few minutes almost all of them were annihilated, and a handful of survivors were pushed back and slashed to death; thousands of our friends became casualties and lost their lives to spare ours.

That afternoon, Joseph, the Wizard butchered 3,333 natives that came to rescue us. It was sad to see the river of blood running around the walls of our house. All our soldiers, who were armed with machetes, log sticks, and shotguns, had fallen, except one who managed to escape alive but severely slashed. The escapee couldn't stand anymore and fell flat on his stomach. Incredibly, he dragged himself under a barbed wire fence to enter a cattle field. In a couple of minutes, he gave up and rested motionless, just waiting to turn his soul to Jus Supp.

John Rudelir came to check on his cattle and spotted the body from a distance. He got off his horse and drew his revolver in self-defense, approaching the strange man laying on the ground. Cautiously, he came close to the body, with his gun in hand, ready to pull the trigger on any suspicious movement. John Rudelir called out to the man to get up; he yelled three times, but the man didn't move or answer back. John Rudelir kicked him a couple of times, and the man moaned in pain.

John Rudelir found out that the man was seriously wounded; he tried to talk to him to get some information before he died.

The man let John know that Dr. Watters was under attack and that he needed help at once. John made a last effort to get more information, but it was too late. In a few seconds, he took his last breath and passed away in the arms of John Rudelir. John got on his horse and went home to warn his brothers to give the peasant a decent burial.

John Rudelir saddled a fresh horse, called Nero, and rode Nero as he was his fastest and favorite horse. He passed by Dr. Watters' house to check it out for himself and to witness and gather information before he went on the road to Sun City. He couldn't believe what he was seeing. Hundreds of dead bodies lay on the roads, and he noticed Joseph, the Wizard walking in all directions to give orders to his evil army. He turned his horse around and went to the dirt road that would take him to Sun City to get help to save Dr. Watters and his family. In a couple of hours, he made it to the outskirts of the famous deserted city. When he was a few minutes away from the Sun City's military base, he started to remember and think about what and how he had to report the urgency of the rescue undertaking. His mind didn't stop thinking about the horde of bodies he had seen piled up, dead, in the dirt roads near Dr. Watters' property, and the one he had found a few hours back in his paddock field, who had died in his arms. He also remembered the dead bodies laying around Dr. Watters' walls. Finally, John Rudelir arrived. Immediately, he was escorted to the commander's office; he took a deep breath and notified the army chief commander about the killing of innocent people, trying to save the lives of Dr. Watters, Zishe, and Mike. Commander Joe Smoke sent a battalion of three hundred soldiers, three tanks, and a chopper for air strike support.

When the troops arrived, Joseph, the Wizard had already fled. He had been warned; a high-ranking informer within the armed forces notified him. The military man freed Dr. Watters and started to pick up human corpses. They dug trenches and holes and tossed all the dead men in the holes and set a fire to burn everyone that had been thrown in the trenches.

AUGUSTUS' LASSO SHOT THE WIZARD

Augustus Lasso, the father of Reigo Lasso, came one night to call Dr. Watters to take him home for his wife was very sick. But on the way to Dr. Watters' home, he ran into Joseph, the Wizard who offered him help; he assured Augustus that he was going to magically heal his wife in no time.

Joseph, the Wizard, convinced Augustus to hire him to treat his wife. They both came into the living room and Joseph, the Wizard convinced Augustus to wait outside for him because he had to pray alone so the spirit of Thunder might cure his wife. Once in the room, he started to chant evil phrases and speak in unknown words; he was making up the ceremony and he began to yell louder to call his demons to intercede. Eventually, he pulled Augustus' wife down from her bed and dragged her onto the floor, then he raped her.

He ran away before Augustus found out and escaped. Augustus gave chase, with seven of his best fearless hitmen, but they couldn't catch him because he hid in the mountains. Augustus kept his people armed and stationed at key points to catch Joseph, the Wizard; he blocked all the roads that connected to the main highway to Sun City. Augustus even had his men poison all the nearby wells, and all the natural water resources: streams, lagoons, waterfalls, and small ponds.

Three days later, Joseph, the Wizard came down from the mountains at night and went into his house to get food supplies and munitions. He was sure he could fool Augustus' people and go back to his hiding place. He sat leaning his back against the trunk of a tall mango tree to wait for his wife and daughters who were cooking and packing food, and other primary supplies, he wanted to take enough to feed him for two weeks. A whistleblower informed Augustus, that Joseph, the Wizard was leaning against a tree; he also told him that Joseph, the Wizard came back from hiding, and he was standing by for food supplies.

Augustus got his rifle ready and loaded it with silver bullets for he had been told that Joseph, the Wizard can only be killed with silver bullets. Silently, he rode his horse and approached cautiously, and when he was at close range, he aimed his weapon and shot him eleven times not missing a single time. He held his rifle up, looking through the scope, and said to himself, *"Eleven silver bullets right in the center of the heart; he's dead for sure!"*

Augustus went back to his house and called his people to keep watch and to remain in their places until they were given new orders. He also had in mind to pass them the good news, that he had already killed Joseph, the Wizard. Augustus was sure that Joseph was dead for no one could survive eleven silver bullets through the heart and the head. He had seen eleven holes in his body when the bullets came out.

Back at Joseph, The Wizard's home, his wife had called Dr. John Barille who came at once to save Joseph, the Wizard. After a quick examination, Dr. Barille's diagnosis was final; Joseph, The Wizard would die within eleven hours. Dr. Barille put bandages soaked in alcohol to cover the holes and to stop the blood from soaking the blankets. That was the end of Joseph, The Wizard everybody thought, except Joseph, The Wizard himself. He knew Thudil, the lord of darkness, wouldn't take him to hell yet. Thudil planned a fake burial for his evil angel here on earth, and to fool everybody, especially to make me, Mike Watters, think that I was a free young man, and I didn't have to fear Joseph, the Wizard anymore.

I FALL IN LOVE

It was in my English class that my eye was caught by Giovanni Conde staring at the most beautiful girl in the entire valley, Betty Schilling, who was beyond my reach, for the following reasons: first, she was the most popular, rich, and famous girl in town, all the wealthy boys challenged each other to get close to her, and I'm talking about hundreds who had asked her out, but she had rejected all of them. She was the daughter of the wealthiest man in town, Mr. Solomon Schilling; he was known by everybody to be corrupt and the cruelest lord that the inhabitants of the valley had seen in the last two centuries. He had tortured and killed hundreds of men, women, and children that wouldn't agree with him.

I met Betty Schilling in my biology class, in the ninth grade. I was left speechless by her beauty and elegance; she had the figure of a model, the face of an angel, and her long natural brown, curly hair hung down to her waist. Her blue eyes were constantly changing to yellow and green with exposure to the light.

I didn't dare to look at her or even say hi, for she was too much for me. I was a poor, shy boy. But all the boys in my class had cash to go around and flirted with her all the time. I looked out the corner of my eye and listened to their conversations, that's all I could hope for. I was surprised because she ignored all of them every time they asked her out. William Commey was considered to be the most handsome boy in the school and also in the Saint Nicholas Valley; he stood six feet four inches tall, was blonde, very muscular, and wealthy. At the end of the class period, he was the last boy to get up and went to meet her; he sat at an empty desk next to her while she was putting books in her satchel. He started talking to her, and I noticed that she didn't reject him.

Instantly, I felt like a sword was piercing my heart, breaking it in half. I couldn't control my emotions and turned my head to watch them. She turned at the same time and saw me. I tried to lower my eyes avoiding a confrontation. I couldn't believe her reaction: she smiled and waved at me!

William noticed and angrily turned to give me a defiant look; he moved his lips and said, "Stop flirting with her, or I'll kill you!" All of the boys and girls that were watching laughed at me and chanted in support of William. The professor dismissed us from our biology class and rushed us out because he was ready to start the next class. I went out quickly and zigged-zagged to avoid running into all the students rushing to get in for the next class period. Next, I had physics with the toughest math teacher I had ever had. In a couple of minutes, I was in and sat at my desk.

Giovanni Conde was following me and came to sit next to me to warn me about William. Conde said, "You can run away, or you can face him and stand up to defend your honor,"

He added, "But remember, if you run, you'll be on the run for the rest of your life." He finished, "Now it is all up to you, a piece of advice I give you, be a man and fight for what's yours. Betty flirted with you, that means she likes you." I nodded and thanked Giovanni Conde for his warning and concern.

I went home that day with a big smile on my face, Zishe asked me, "Why are you so happy?' I hesitated to answer. She said, ' Don't worry it's fine to fall in love for the first time and it's wonderful, I can read it in your eyes. Who is the lucky young lady?" Because I hesitated to reply, she asked me again.

I answered her very happily, "Betty Schilling." Zishe's face changed from happiness to sadness; I knew she became worried about me as soon as she heard Miss Schilling's name.

The next day, I woke up forty-five minutes earlier than usual; I spent a long time getting dressed and combing my long hair. I never have used gel, but this morning I made an exception and fixed up my long, dark black, curly hair with a lot of grease. I was falling in love for the first time, and I had to impress Betty.

I went to my first class looking cool. Giovanni Conde was impressed and complimented me. William came in as usual dressed elegantly, but this time trying to get me in trouble. He was working hard to charm Betty even if he had to punch me in the nose; everybody knew he was going to end up with her, it was just a matter of time. The class started, but Betty hadn't come in yet. The teacher was already calling the last name on the roll when the door popped open and it was Betty coming in late. She came in with a big smile and apologized to the professor. All the boys and girls stared at her and giggled among themselves.

William invited her to come and sit next to him; she refused the invitation and made eye contact with me with a sweet smile. I smiled back at her. She sat next to Sylvia Fyffer. Sylvia was a beautiful, blonde girl with amazing curly, long hair, and was the most popular girl in the entire valley and was known as Sylvia, the Piper because her body had the shape of a pipe and two of her brothers used to smoke pot in pipes. Indeed, I couldn't control my excitement because everybody kept an eye on me. My best friend, Giovanni Conde, patted my back, and William slammed his fist on the desk and pointed his finger at me.

At ten minutes to two in the afternoon, we were dismissed for the day. I was walking down the street with Joe Anderson, the only black kid in a white-only school, and he was in the 10th grade, and all my classes. Because he was black, they bullied him harshly; everyone called him nasty names, and he used to tell me that I was the only one that treated him with respect and didn't make remarks because of the color of his skin.

Betty was talking with Crystal, Sylvia, and Carolina, and they were walking sixty feet behind us. We could hear them laughing out loud and yelling to get the attention of all the boys going back to their homes. Ten minutes later, we split, and everyone went to their homes. Crystal yelled at me to wait for her. We walked together the rest of the way since we lived on the same block. I had a long conversation with her in front of her house.

Time went by quickly, and she raised her left arm to look at the time on her wristwatch, "Oh my God! 43 minutes we've been gossiping, and I'm starving! I need to get inside, or my mom will kill me!" I opened the fancy gate for her to go into the front yard. She waved me goodbye, and I was about 35 feet away from the gate when I heard her voice calling me to come back. I turned around and went to the metal fence gate. I grabbed one of the iron bars with my hands lifted and stood on my toes. She placed one hand on my right bicep, pressed her thumb on it, then started talking. I gotta tell you, something special happened on the way to the last class period that afternoon. I just nodded without saying a word.

Crystal began with a smile from ear to ear, "I was talking to Sylvia, Carolina, and Betty, and we were having a cool chat about all the guys in Sun City school; we started asking questions like whose the most handsome? We all agreed that William takes the first place. And the second one goes to ..." she took a long pause, "The second goes to ..." she took a long pause again, "... to Dr. Watters' son!" I was shaking and nervous when she told me, the girls had picked me as the second-most handsome boy in the Sun City school district. "But that's the second piece of gossip I'm telling you; the cool one is this, and it's all about William, Conde, and you." She stopped for a long time to keep me interested. I wanted to know so badly, but she didn't start telling me, instead she changed the subject for a couple of minutes to torture me mentally for a long time. I had no choice but to beg her to tell me right away; I was ready to fall on my knees, but she chose to share her secret with me.

She started with a loud "Yeah, Sylvia Piper asked every one of us about what boy we wanted to date. Caroline answered quickly; she said that she would love to go out with Giovanni Conde. Of course, The Piper girl gave us a unique piece of information about her sentimental inclination which was directing her heart. She told us that she was interested in William and that she was going to prepare and mend her nets to fish him out, even from the deepest and cold waters in the Pacific Ocean." She was silent for a good fifty-five seconds again, and I was eager to hear the whole tale, and for her to finish the story. I had no idea that this time, I was going to be the hero. She stalled for three seconds, then she carried on with the information; indeed, she kept me very nervous as the waiting was killing me. I didn't want to push her, and I waited very patiently. The truth is, it was hard to control my emotions, but in the end, I made the right choice to stand by for her to tell me the end of this interesting yarn. By and by, she made it known to me and told me the last piece, which changed my life. Definitely, I was destined to become the coolest and the luckiest kid in the valley of the sun!

She started by giving me a pat on my back and a peck on my cheek, "I'm in love with Mike Watters, he's so cool and he has a heart of an angel.' Truly, that's what Betty Schilling told us." I lowered my head and prayed in my mind to thank God for giving me my first girl, not just a girl, but the best girl in town. I knew I had to fight and shed blood to stay by her side. The day before, my friend, Conde had encouraged me to keep an eye open and to prepare myself for war against William and anybody else who came to fight me.

On Friday of that same week, my friend Giovanni Conde and all the boys went home to Saint Nicholas Village for the weekend. As usual, Zishe asked me about my beloved Betty when I got to her room; she wanted me to tell her everything about me and Betty. I told her about my happiness in a couple of minutes. She celebrated with me, but she shared her concerns and warned me to be careful.

The weekend sped past, and I left the house at 4:15 AM on Monday, to make it in time to my first class. The drive was about two hours long to Sun City because it was in December during the rainy season. The dirt road was flooded and muddy, and the bus had to drive slowly and at times wait for brook currents to become shallow for the old vehicle to cross over log bridges.

Finally, I arrived and went straight to the school; the school guard opened the gate, and all the students rushed to the first class period. Betty was the first to come in; she saw an empty double seat in the first row, and she sat in one and laid a book and her purse on the other desk to reserve it for her friend, Sylvia Piper. The desk was to her left because her friend, Piper, was running late. The boys wanted to take the seat she had reserved but she didn't allow them to. I walked in, and she noticed me. My heart was pounding since Crystal had told me that Betty liked me.

I passed by to take an available seat in the back row. It was a bombshell to me! My eyes opened wide when she moved the books she had on top of the desk she had reserved, and to my surprise, she asked me if I wanted to sit next to her. William was coming in and saw the whole thing he was left fuming and forced me to come to blows to protect myself. He pushed me to the wall and slammed me on the chalkboard. He wrapped his hands tightly around my throat and picked me up by my neck as easily as lifting a rooster. All the students cheered "William, William, William…" Fortunately, Professor Ralph Faggiolli arrived and put a stop to the fight. I was certain Goliath was trying to put an end to my life, had not the professor walked in, in the nick of time to save my life.

The school year ended, and I was deeply in love, but my lass was going to be a long way from me during the vacation. I knew she had fallen in love with me, and I wanted to be with her for the rest of my life. But the truth is, I couldn't stay with her because on the first day of the next school year, I was going to find out she would move to a bigger private school in Eternal City, the most important city in the country. I ran into her a year later when I was trudging on the main street, downtown in the city she had moved to, attending the famous private college. That was going to be the end of my high school sweetheart my mind was telling me. I would never see or hear of her ever again.

I GOT TIPSY

I thought about the night I got drunk with Giovanni Conde. I was happy that I had had my first date with Betty Schilling, the cutest, richest, and hottest girl in the school. It had been three days ago when I got my first kiss ever, and I shared my joy with my best friend, Conde. He suggested we go out and celebrate; he thought to have a few shots of rum. We picked a place; we both agreed to go to the King's Pub. Conde had been there many times, but I had never been in a pub, in fact, I had never tried a sip of any alcoholic drink in my life.

Our classmates, Axel Faggiolli, and my foe, William Commey, were already drinking beers when we arrived there. Commey gave me the evil eye, signaled with his finger pointing to the door, and mouthed the words "get lost."

Conde saw it and told me that we were going to stay, no matter what, and not to be afraid; he also gave Commey the middle finger, and told him, "*You* go to hell!" Conde said that I needed to say no, sometimes if I wanted to be unchained for the rest of my life. I needed to stand up for my rights and fight to be regarded with greater respect.

We talked for a couple of hours, and I swigged three glasses of rum. Conde drank three glasses of vodka and a shot of Mexican Tequila. I felt completely giddy; I stood up to go take a pee, and I wobbled so badly that before I got to the restroom I fell over chairs and tables. Conde dashed to assist me. Faggiolli and Commey were laughing at me and they kept calling me nasty names.

Conde grabbed me by my right hand, led me out of the building, and escorted me five blocks to the shores of the Salt Brook. I felt like I was going to die! The moon was spinning around, and the streets were not flat, but they were built up and down going all the way to the blue sky. I shouted and moaned, desperately. I promised myself, *"If I get my body and mind back to normal, I will never drink a single sip of alcohol for the rest of my life!"*

I spoke out so loudly, that Conde was laughing, and I barely heard him say, "I said those words the first time I got drunk!" He came closer, and whispered, "I have done it about one hundred times since the first time. What I'm trying to say is that we always break our promises." I just listened, making sure no sound came out of my mouth; I thought, *I will keep my promise.* I puked all over myself and fell asleep for thirty-three minutes.

Conde took me safely till near to my house and then went on his way. I got in quietly, sick and ashamed of myself.

CRAZY ISAIAH BURNS
IT ALL

My mind was taking me back to the night Crazy Isaiah wanted to set me on fire. My ugly, fat cousin, Isaiah, was hired by Joseph, the Wizard to set me and all my belongings on fire. The plan was to burn me alive. Joseph, the Wizard was informed that Isaiah didn't like me one bit and that he would kindle me for peanuts or a fistful of pennies.

The reason he hated me so much was that I was an honors student, and he was my classmate. All the students in my class respected me, and they loved my work ethic and my sense of style; of course, all of them knew I was the only son of Dr. Watters. From the age of five, I didn't follow the street gang, but Dr. Watters's leadership, especially, Zishe's teachings. I had become a good listener, and the only street leader I had followed was myself.

I was a unique writer and an excellent poet. And I got the knack of it more and more with every single school year, and Isaiah envied me, and Prince Demon, Isaiah had endless infernal jealousy toward me. He had wanted to get rid of me a long time ago. And, I was sure, he would not stop and hoped to torture me. I had told Dr. Watters that I didn't want to live in his house anymore because he was up to something to harm me. Dr. Watters didn't bother to find a different place for me. He thought I was safe at Aunt Matilda's lodging place in Sun City because she was his best friend, and he had entrusted me in her care. I got tired of Isaiah insulting me at home, and in school because we were attending the same school and were in the same grade.

One morning at recess, I saw a familiar individual. He was standing adjacent to the wired fence outside the school. Isaiah was walking toward the old man; it was very weird to see him exchanging words with Joseph, the Wizard! They were aware that I was staring at them. I didn't hear their conversation because I was about six hundred feet away. But their meeting was brief, and Isaiah looked nervous as he walked away slowly, his head hanging, before waving goodbye to Joseph, the Wizard. He kept turning his head around to make sure no one was watching him talking to Joseph, the Wizard, the most fearful, satanic man in the whole world.

Isaiah always talked trash about me; he gossiped to Gramma and Dad and made nasty accusations toward me, just to get me in trouble. He spread rumors in school that we were so poor and that we lived like pigs in the smallest village in the huge Saint Nicholas Green Valley, along the banks of the Saint Nicholas River Territory. Of course, the students didn't believe him because he had been diagnosed as mentally ill a few years back. and since then, he was known as Crazy Isaiah. His hate for me was out of this world, and he wouldn't dither to stab me in the back the first chance that he got.

One weekend I went back to Saint Nicholas to visit Zishe and go fishing to feed her. Dr. Watters was angry at me. He was, as usual, working in his lab. But as soon as he heard me talking to Zishe, he came out to admonish me. He notified me that Isaiah had let him know that his mother, Matilda, told him to inform Dr. Watters that I was doing drugs, smoking marijuana, and cigarettes, and also snorting cocaine. But, Dr. Watters added that she had also informed him that I was hooked on shooting up heroine! Dr. Watters threatened me with canceling my education if he found out that Matilda wasn't lying about the matter; he said he was going to do his own investigation.

Of course, I knew Crazy Isaiah was determined to get my back up against the wall, as I had seen him talking to Joseph, the Wizard, so, I had the evidence at hand. Everything made sense; Crazy Isaiah had been working with the devil, but I didn't dare to tell Dr. Watters, as he wouldn't believe me. I needed to ask Zishe to talk to Leerd to help me out in a supernatural way, as he had done in the past on multiple occasions.

A few days went by, and I was thinking about how to tell Dr. Watters that I was not on drugs. Luckily for me, my request and prayers were going to be answered in a very short time.

Mary Ann, Crazy Isaiah's little sister came running to hug me on a Monday morning when I was coming back from Saint Nicholas Village after spending the weekend with Zishe. She was waiting for her sugar candy because I used to bring her some goodies every time I came back from visiting Zishe. I pretended I didn't have anything for her, and in a fake voice, I said, "Hello, Mary Ann. I forgot your sugar-candy cane. I'm sorry!" As I said, Mary Ann was one of Isaiah's younger sisters. She walked away head hanging down, and nearly in tears, so I called her back, as I already had the candy in my hand. I gave it to her, and she stretched her arm out and grabbed the candy, and put out her long, skinny fingers to take a couple of fruits she saw in my backpack, as well. She looked around to make sure no one was watching us, then she delved inside my backpack, for she was trying to tell me a secret.

I went to my room, opened the door, and went in. I wasn't aware that she had been following me the whole time. I tried to close the door behind me, but Mary Ann was holding it and pushing to open it before I turned on the light. I noticed her and let her in with me. She was already sucking the candy and already telling me what she knew about Crazy Isaiah. I smelled that something had been burned inside my room and ashes were flying into my eyes, nose, and mouth; up till then, I hadn't noticed anything because Mary Ann had stopped me from flipping out.

I was about to turn the light switch on, but Mary Ann brought me to an abrupt halt and said, "No, Mike, don't turn it on yet; I got to tell you something first!" She took a long pause, then, spoke as softly as she could. It was clear she knew somebody might be trying to listen to our conversation. She shook her head, and finally, she told me Isaiah and a weird guy, dressed in a camouflage uniform and holding many weapons, were in my room on Saturday. She continued, still looking around, and said, "The strange fellow told Isaiah, 'Make Mike's life miserable; attack his spirit and material possessions, but don't put an end to him yet. Thudil, my boss doesn't want him dead yet.'" She also informed me, that the weird man told Isaiah, "Today, I want you to burn his clothes, books, and everything he owns related to his school."

I stopped her and turned on the light to see the mess with my own eyes. I was crying and devastated as it was almost the end of the school year, and all my notes and books had been burned. Mary Ann was crying, and she kept telling me how Crazy Isaiah and Joseph, the Wizard were having a good time burning my room. She said they kindled and burned everything in the room, using matches, and a lighter they were using to light a bunch of cigars they kept rolling up. Mary Ann brought an end to the awful event telling me to be careful because Isaiah answered the weird guy, "I'll do whatever you ask me to, Joseph, the Wizard. Just let me know when, where, what, and how you want me to torment him."

The rumors were spreading fast in the school. An anonymous student even posted a note on the school bulletin board, which said, "Beware! Crazy Isaiah is losing his marbles again!" Luckily, I got tremendous support from my classmates; some of them bought me new books, and others helped me to get notes and rewrite them in brand-new notebooks. And that same year, I moved out of Matilda's boarding place. At the very end of the school year, Isaiah falsely accused me a few more times of a couple of crimes, but Leerd shielded my body and spirit from falling into the hands of Joseph, the Wizard's evil plot.

SPEEDY THOMAS FALLING DEEP

Thomas, the tailor, was riding his old, rusty 1950 Oldsmobile, two-door, jet back Model 88. He was on his way back to Saint Nicolas Village. It was late Friday, and I was going back home to spend the weekend with Zishe, to take care of her, and provide a fresh fish supply for at least a month. The sun was high up in the blue sky, and it was magically balmy, and around 3:33 P.M. I was soaked from the heat and humidity that made me sweat like a pig.

Thomas, the tailor sped up in his Oldsmobile and screeched the rear tires to blow dust on me. I was sure he did it on purpose! The grime was all over me; he caught me as he passed by and backed the car up to take a look at me; I was splashed with mud from head to toe, which left me blind and deaf for a good three minutes. Thomas, the tailor stopped about 100 yards away from me again and asked me to get in. I couldn't sit in the car because there was no room; he had a bunch of tools, boxes, and rolls of colorful fabrics, to make uniforms for graduation in the local elementary school, so, I stood instead. His, son Sam was in the passenger seat peeling and eating a banana.

Thomas drove up the hill and stopped on the plateau to check the engine that was overheating. I had been taking a long nap while he was checking the car, and I didn't bother to open my eyes. Suddenly, I heard Thomas talking to a familiar voice. I opened my eyes to take a look and I was in shock when I saw him having a long talk with Joseph, the Wizard. I didn't perceive, clearly, what they were talking about, but I was sure they were talking about me. And for sure, it was an evil plan they had in mind, and they were going to set the plot in motion. After I saw them shaking hands, I knew that I couldn't trust Thomas, but I kept praying to Jus Supp, the Lord of Goodness, to send Leerd to rescue me; I was meditating a lot on what to do in case of an emergency. Thomas came back, sat in behind the old dusty wheel, and turned the switch to start up the tarnished engine, which took a couple of minutes to start up. Thomas grabbed the gear lever, changed to first gear, and off we went. He reached 50 miles an hour, going down the steep, dirt road; he was on a suicidal mission, according to my thinking!

He slowed down a bit to tell his son to take off his seat belt to jump out of the car. It took no time for his son to jump because by now, the car was already flying about three hundred feet high in the air. I got goosebumps and closed my eyes. I sensed a light beam covering my body. I opened my eyes a few seconds later and saw the car in slow motion, descending and halfway to hitting the gigantic, sharp, pyramid-shaped rocks. I looked down to the bottom of the canyon. I was standing at the edge of the cliff on the dusty main road; I still saw Leerd speeding away like a rocket, up into a single cloud, still going up and almost touching heaven's door. In a split second, he entered heaven's door and vanished from sight. Of course, I was the only one who had seen him. Immediately, I turned to watch the car still free-falling, and I kept staring at it. I saw a body diving from one of the doors and landing on a thick pile of dried grass that had been collected to feed a herd of cows, mooing, and watching the scene of the car going down over their heads.

I waited for about five seconds, to see the vehicle hammering the rocks as soon as it made contact with the rocky ground. It shattered and a column of smoke reached an immeasurable altitude. But, a second before, the car had landed in a tree, cutting several branches, like a sharp, motorized saw. Thomas had been holding tight to the steering wheel; the car flipped over and sent him through a hole created by his head and hit the already damaged windshield.

I fell on my knees to say a brief prayer for a few minutes. And I ran down the steep dusty road for 5 miles, to make it to Saint Nicholas Village. I couldn't clear my mind of the horrific scene of Thomas and his son falling, using his car roof as a parachute. I was one hundred percent sure they had died instantly.

I went into my room, put my backpack away, and rushed to the lab to tell Dr. Watters to be prepared for Thomas' funeral.

Meanwhile, at the scene of the lethal accident, firefighters from Sun City had arrived five minutes earlier. Three brave firefighters were going down on three ropes to get to the bottom and pick up the two dead bodies. News spread fast, and in seconds, the rescue team waited at the top, including all the medical personnel and equipment operators. The rescue team was surrounded by bystanders that came out from nearby villages. Police officers were working hard to keep onlookers away from the restricted area. All the people were eager to see the bodies being lifted with the ropes.

It was a miracle; a lady holding her twin girls, screamed when she saw Tomas' son gripping the rope, showing only a few minor cuts and scratches on his arms. It was Joseph, the Wizard who carried him in his arms to set him on the dried cow manure.

An old lady walking with the support of a wooden, handmade cane, yelled from the other side. "I saw him with my own two blind eyes!" she assured the crowd.

They all laughed and chanted, "Long live Joseph, the Wizard!" Sam was physically evaluated; the medics didn't find any severe injury. The rescue mission squad asked Sam several questions, but he refused to answer any, he just nodded and shook his head to reply to all of them.

Back in the village, I went to the stream to swim in the fishpond. I spent about an hour swimming and diving. I didn't notice that Joseph, the Wizard was watching me, while sitting on a rock, on the tallest hill in the middle of the valley. He didn't dare attack me! Perhaps he was surprised that the plot between him and Thomas to kill me in the car accident, had failed. Perhaps he knew it wasn't going to work or he was having fun watching me swimming and diving.

My swimming and diving were now over; I got dressed to start fishing. I caught a bunch of fish in about thirty minutes. I was happy with the catch and went home. I ran into a group of old ladies gossiping about the car accident Thomas had been in, a few hours ago. Some of them said that he and Sam were alive, and others said that Joseph, the Wizard had rescued them. They saw me and told me that everyone in the village thought I had died in the car wreckage. They added that they hadn't found my body dead or alive, but the paramedics and firefighters had found and rescued Thomas and Sam, safe and sound; they had suffered only minor cuts and scratches. I didn't say a word; I just happily smiled at them and waved them goodbye. I ran into my house looking for and calling out to Zishe.

The group of old ladies followed me for a couple of blocks, tittle-tattling behind me, asking the following question, "Is it true that Joseph, the Wizard had saved you with his magic wand?"

THE SEVENTH SACRED HATCH

Lord Jus Supp had held a hasty, divine summit with his unswerving son, Leerd, to entrust him with a very tough quest. And Jus Supp sent him down to planet Earth to have a top-secret meeting with me.

He came down, walking in a human's physical body; he was walking with his bare feet on a million shining rainbow-colored roads and diamond-paved paths near to where his majesty, Lord Jus Supp's dwelling and vacationing place was located, here on earth; this special place was secured with seven invisible spiritual forces, for Jus Supp and Leerd to come down to earth and to go up into heaven.

But we mortals were not allowed to see the secret entrances because they were set aside for Jus Supp and Leerd only. But, I'd been chosen, and I was walking on the same road Leerd was on; I was gathering leaves for Zishe's natural medicinal drink, not knowing that it was hallowed ground. It was the first and only time I saw, talked, and walked with Leerd in his human form.

Leerd walked, moved his lips, and with no sound, he mouthed to me, "You're favored; look at the palm of your hands; three straight lines. That means you're unique, and that's the reason you've been chosen. You'll become a superhero, and you, Mike Watters, will be known as MegAm, short for Mega American." He shared the mission his father, Lord Jus Supp had enjoined him to pass down to me. Leerd also said, "Today, I'll allow you to see me going through the seven angelic guarded doors; of course, it will be a vision of the seven gates that I'm going to go through to get back to Jus Supp's dwelling place." And so, he strolled to the first door:

FIRST DOOR: He banged with the back of his right hand at the first of seven doors because he needed to enter right away.

And before going into the first door, he looked at me, and before he went back to the throne of Jus Supp, he said, "Don't forget, you've been chosen." He was still talking when the invisible gate opened. Leerd let me see all of them with my own physical eyes. And when they opened, Leerd moved forward; all of a sudden, a strong wind struck and shook him; he stopped the gray mist, and colorful clouds that built a roof over his head to block the burning fire that burst into flames; everything and everyone who dared to enter the first door to the center of the universe where Jus Supp resided, was burned to the ground.

But Jus Supp commanded his invisible guardian angels to halt the wind, put out the fire, and make a tunnel for Leerd to proceed. And Leerd went on his way to the second gate. He traveled a long distance, strolling in the clouds. All of the sudden, he was banging at the second door.

SECOND DOOR: I was authorized to watch Leerd's fights to enter the door. A tsunami of swords floated in the high tide of hot water, moving in different directions, cutting and burning everything they touched. Again, Jus Supp ordered his exclusive guardian army to stop the hurricane and to secure a safe entrance to Leerd. I heard Jus Supp speak in a thunderously loud voice, ordering the tsunami to form a tunnel for Leerd, and to give him a safe pass to advance to the third secret gate. Immediately, the tide levels lowered to the ground and turned into a magic flying carpet; Leerd stepped on it and traveled the rest of the way to door number three. He straddled the gigantic, tsunami blanket defending his prone body.

THIRD DOOR: Leerd sauntered into the forest, looking for a cool spot to rest, and he found shade under a huge star sapling dancing over his head. A flock of angelic birds flew over and serenaded him with a repertoire of heavenly hymns. He laid down for about three minutes; the resting time was enough that he could get back on his feet, full of energy, and move forward. He knew he had to be ready and wary about the danger and jump and tear down the unseen walls that guarded and protected the very next door that stood strong and tall, about three hundred feet ahead of him.

Leerd stopped, stared, and stood closer, a few feet from the third door. He smelled ashes, felt heat, and a flame of fire ignited, blowing out of the door, eleven feet high from the ground, but not burning anymore. The smoke stopped and formed a wall, impossible to climb or go through. He turned himself into a human figure shadow to fight because he had to go through the seven secret forces as a human before finishing the earthly mission. Leerd knelt and asked for approval from

Jus Supp in a three-holy-word prayer. A magic force tore down the strange wall and turned it into a huge, red, long sponge. He waited a few seconds to step onto it. A tall whirlwind landed on top of it and built a funnel that connected it to the sun. Instantly, the red carpet was transformed into a mile-long, white, snow sponge. Leerd ran to it, dug a hole in the snow, and went in.

He sat inside the long, white snow road which slowly melted and became a long, narrow river for Leerd to swim in the rest of the way; it went all the way to the fourth door's entrance. The piece of snow where Leerd was standing, didn't melt but built a snowman mold to fit him into, so he kept the human figure shadow of a snowman.

THE FOURTH DOOR: Thudil showed up in human form as soon as the river dried up, and left Leerd laying on the dusty ground. Leerd and Thudil's shadows engaged in a one-on-one fight. The fight became a fearful battle between the two titans, Leerd, the Celestial Lord, and Thudil, the Lord of Hellfire engaged in a nasty battle; they were using all kinds of bizarre galactic weapons and mystical gadgets, and they changed and replaced them every second. In the end, they wrestled to the death and finished the duel in less than a second.

Leerd celebrated, and Thudil, the loser, retreated, screaming in pain and cursing. Finally, Leerd moved forward to the next door. He started a light rain, and a rainbow formed, picked him up, and swallowed him, sending him to the other end to drop him off at the next door. Leerd rode on to the top of the rainbow's arch and arrived at the fifth door in a split second.

THE FIFTH DOOR: The rainbow's two legs were pinned to the ground, next to the fifth door. It tilted to slide Leerd to the right end. He read the sign and the arrow that showed the way to go to the fifth door's access. At this moment, everything seemed hushed, and around the road, everything was waiting to proceed. He advanced, not aware of where and when the attack would come. Suddenly, he noticed something fishy and stopped to put his ideas together and to come up with a good plan to protect himself and escape. A whistle blew and he started to hear the sound of a thunderous alarm; the blowing was so loud that he fell on the ground and covered his ears with dried leaves he'd picked up from the ground.

The whistling carried on, and a multitude of silver shining trumpets flew around sounding even louder than the whistle that had started to blast in his ears. The trumpets were shooting poisonous darts out of their funnels, and all were aimed at Leerd's head and chest. A tenor voice sang, "Death to Leerd, death to Leerd! Shoot to kill him!" Leerd rolled on the dust in pain; in a second, he stopped moving, and the shower of darts was piling up on him, building a mountain that grew taller and taller by the second. The battle ended soon, and to me, that was the end of Leerd's existence as the Guardian of the Shappa Galaxy. A cool breeze blew gently from the West and swept away the poisonous darts to clean the mess; now the mountain leveled off in a split second.

Jus Supp ordered bees to come to the rescue. He also commanded them to sting Leerd's body, but not his temples because, he was not dead; he sent signals to remove all the venom from his body, and Jus Supp spoke loudly and clearly. He added to his dialogue, "He must live for my name's sake and the sake of planet Earth. Surely, he'll live, and he will carry my message to the land of the free, which is the home of the wise." The bees rushed to land on his almost-dead body to save the still-human angel that Lord Jus Supp needed to carry out his mission, for he still needed to cross two more sacred gates to become a full spirit and enter into Jus Supp's territory.

Leerd crossed the gate flown by the colony of bees and went to the other side. He gained consciousness a few seconds later.

THE SIXTH DOOR: An enormous ophidian slithered sideways without moving forward. Evidently, it was guarding and watching the sixth door's entrance. The long, hand-thick reptile was also seducing a young woman, covering only her private parts with a snakeskin miniskirt; she was, in turn, whistling and singing to charm the creepy creature. The long neck of the serpent dropped, bumping its huge head on the ground; she took a short nap, then it lifted its head; she went back to taking naps every minute. A barefoot, naked boy was arguing and fighting with his older brother, who looked a thousand years younger than his scared, scarred, and wrinkled-faced brother; the older one stroked his long, narrow beard and charged at his sibling with a heavy stone ax. He split his body into two pieces, as easily as hewing a piece of hardwood log with a chainsaw. The left part of his body showed that his heart was still hanging and beating very slowly; he was screaming to get the attention of the woman who was only focused on taking care of the snake.

He yelled, over and over, apparently calling his mom, saying, "Mom, please help me; my brother is beating me to death. " Taking his last breath he said, "I am dying." Instantly, the snake fell asleep one more time, and Leerd ran at full speed to enter the sixth door.

THE SEVENTH DOOR: Leerd arrived at the last door. A sweet voice gave him a warm welcome to the last door's entrance, the road to Jus Supp's paradise. Here's where the most honorable maker of all the planets and the creator of the universe dwells. Jus Supp lives forever and ever on the other side of the seventh door. A handsome young man, elegantly dressed in white, came to meet Leerd to escort him back to his eternal home.

He introduced himself as I was still watching Leerd trekking; he told me, "I'm the only son of Jus Supp, the Supreme Master of the Galaxies, and I blindly trust and obey my father: he's the creator of everything you see and don't see." The elegant boy said, "Now, I'll escort you to your father. This day will be written in the history books, now please follow me with your eyes wide open."

Leerd then said to me, "And, this was the last vision I let you see." Without further ado, Leerd strolled behind Nity, the servant and driver of his flying chariot; I felt I could trust him, and I was comfortably watching his departure from my planet because he was entering the most sacred place in the whole universe.

Leerd was taken up before me, and he stopped talking to me; I just saw a beam of light going up at a high speed; it touched heaven's door in a split second. I stared at the fluorescent beam of light, as I waved goodbye to Leerd strolling in the clouds. And he knew I would never see him again. I jumped to avoid getting hit by objects falling from the highest mountain peaks. Suddenly, a pair of invisible strings lifted Leerd in front of me. He let me watch the divine structure of the heavenly buildings; he dropped a pair of hawsers; I picked them up and went back home.

JOSEPH, THE WIZARD MEETS UP WITH THUDIL

Joseph, the Wizard strode up the hill to get to the top of the tallest mountain range. He stopped and inhaled some air to get the strength to march up the rest of the way. He urgently had to shimmy up to the top of the cliff at the edge of the loneliest, scariest spot in this universe. He sang through his speech to pass it down to Thudil who was standing by for him inside the Ingress Iron Mark Lair. Joseph, the Wizard was walking several feet away from the sinister cave.

He crossed the threshold, and the shadows of wild and vicious animals roared as they pounced on him, and ghosts moved close to lure him to their satanic burrow. Tens of thousands of legions of demons tormented him physically and mentally. In a split second, a rolling, fiery hail star fell from heaven's paneling and chased away the awful creatures. Joseph, the Wizard enjoined them to be gone, with a lion's roar. Immediately, he turned into a lion; a couple of seconds later, he went back to his original human form. Soon after, the star was disabled and landed on his head; it was supporting Joseph, the Wizard's head, temporarily. It was blinding his vision with a dark shadow that was shielding his eyes. He had never imagined losing his eyesight; Joseph, the Wizard had poked out the eyes of hundreds of victims, but no one had touched or caused harm to his eyesight.

Thirty-three minutes later, he met up with Thudil. The questioning began as planned; Thudil transformed himself into a legion of ghosts in one body and flew to a throne made with rotten, calcined clay placed in a gutter, half full of dead rotting flesh mixed with a stinky yellow liquid.

Thudil pointed to a ring of fire next to a burning furnace. Then, Thudil mandated, "That's your future seat for eternity. Thank you for your faithful service, and to reward you for your service to my cause, I grant you that fancy burning ring." He then said, jokingly, "I warn you, your ring chair is very hot, and the heat might cook you alive, and I might taste your flesh for supper!"

The evil Thudil became angry, and Joseph, the Wizard looked him straight in his terrorizing, ghostly eyes. He saw terror and destruction in Thudil's dark face.

He uttered a question that Joseph, the Wizard wasn't prepared to answer. And, the question was, "Why have you failed in my command to make Mike's life hell, here on earth's rocky, green soil? Don't you realize, he must endure agony both physically and spiritually? If he pulls through, he'll turn into a powerful superhero, and spoil my almost-perfect conspiracy. Eventually, if we let him become a superhero, he will rescue all the brats on earth. I want to get into these children's minds so they adore me, and I can take them away from their Lord Jus

Supp's love, care, and protection. They must turn into thieves, killers, liars, and haters, so they may enter into the darkness of the Demons' Ingress Iron Mark Cave, to live and enjoy the fire parade with me, forever. I don't want to have only a few souls with me, burning forever!" Yelling in a thunderous voice, Thudil sounded defiant and challenging, "Stop Zishe's prophesy, and that's an order!"

Joseph, the Wizard took a step back, but his head was spinning in terror, and he was muttering his sad, imaginary thoughts. He plucked up the courage to ask a question, and he said, "What about me? Are you bringing me here to tell me, don't be mean? I don't want to dwell eternally in this dark cave!" Joseph, the Wizard carried on with, "This is not paradise; when you proffered me for this job, I mean, the first time you talked to me, you promised me good times if I joined your team. You lied to me! You promised me joy, happiness, fame, and wealth; you're a liar!"

Thudil replied, "Of course, that's why they call me the inventor of fibs or the father of all lies; even Jus Supp's 'Wise Book' says that I'm the master of disguises and lies!"

Joseph, the Wizard, shuddering and mumbling in a broken voice, said, "I wish to retire, sir!"

Thudil said, "A rejoinder? Not allowed; too late now!" Thudil continued, "You've already sold your soul to me, and there's no way back; just hang on tight, the flame will be hot for you and me both when Jus Supp decides to take away our reign, but now, let's have a good time, with no worries! And when he sends us to that infamous furnace, I'll wipe your tears. We'll weep inside that hot furnace together. Please be patient and enjoy bringing more stupid souls to this place of everlasting torment. They'll be burning in this cave with you and me, for eternity. We don't want to be alone; what do you say?

"We chose to be demons, and this is the reward we'll get at the end; it is a fiery hell that awaits us. That's why I want to round up all the souls still living on earth to come to me, and finally, finally, all of us will end in this horrific burning space. But I have laid my eyes on somebody dear and special to me, and I have set my rat trap for him; his name's Mike Watters. I want him here, even if don't get millions of regular souls. Jus Supp has chosen him to fight against me, and Leerd has planned a special mission for him. He is chosen to become a human angel, and Zishe is his shield. Jus Supp has hired Leerd, his only twin being, to take good care of Mike Watters; he'll protect him, and in a short while, he is going to give him supernatural powers, and I will not be able to touch him. We must move fast, steal his vest suit and stop him from getting supernatural powers. I'm afraid I'm running out of time.

"Listen, your mission is to eliminate the old lady, Zishe, so we can finish him off. I have been informed that she has special powers and a magic wand that Leerd has provided her, to protect Mike and defend herself. It's an order! I want you to go and wipe her out, once and for all. She's on my wanted list, and I need her out of the way, not to get in my way! She must die to clear the way, so it will be easy to get to Mike. The only chance we have to win this dirty battle is to stop her magic wand and do away with her. She praises Leerd every time she lays her hand on the famous and mysterious stick. Don't waste time. Go now! I want results or I'll charge you with my rule of law. I'll break your bones without leniency if you fail! This is the most important mission I have given you; fight with passion and poise to the end, and win or you're doomed, and your own life's on the line!"

LEERD'S MISSION

A day before Leerd came down to talk with me, he was dropped by unseen beings, lowering the cables over the roof of Jus Supp palace. The ceiling cracked and opened the roof for Leerd to land on the floor in front of a golden throne where Lord Jus Sup was sitting. Leerd walked backward because he was not allowed to see Jus Supp face-to-face without burning to ashes instantly. Jus Supp's shining face and body gradually faded away, and soon was covered with a white bail curtain. Then, Jus Supp spoke to Leerd face-to-face. Leerd respectfully listened to Jus Supp, and in a unique way, Leerd saluted Jus Supp with a military-style salute, then he did obeisance to him.

He knelt, and Jus Supp revealed his beatific plan. He sent Leerd visible waves carrying the sound of his voice. He spoke, "I'm sending you again to that special point that I have placed in the middle of all the galaxies that I have created. I have built it in a very special way, but I have also created a bunch of rebellious and disobedient beings. They are corrupt and turning into monsters; they're becoming so mean and corrupt that I want to change my laws to wipe them from the face of the earth, but due to my covenant with them, I cannot modify my statutes, laws, and ordinances.

"This point I have named Oxi, also known as point Earth. I receive a lot of complaints about the killings and corruption. I'm sad and angry, but I love this point so much that I am willing to give them a second chance. I have found a lad that loves me; he's very obedient and he loves to meditate, pray, and ask me for forgiveness and help, not only for himself but also for others. He's a trustworthy boy. I want you to go there and give him supernatural powers to save the Earth, my favorite vacationing point."

Jus Supp summed it up; he said, "I will choose two of my most forthright, and trustworthy servants to go with you on this urgent mission. Soon after you set foot on Point Earth's soil, you are to immediately call the three wise SOS Lords, who are aware of the mission: they're the three wise sons of Sun. So, I have determined, and I will choose you to go to that galaxy now, and you will go again a second time within twelve months to make the right choice."

Jus Supp stated, "Son, I trust you for this mission. I am counting on you: your training, knowledge, and abilities will help you properly train the lad at Oxi point so he can start his mission. Mike Watters is the chosen lad, and I have decided to choose him for this special mission. You must properly bestow him with this new hero's name; he should be called, 'MegAm.'"

Leerd bowed, and after listening to him, he went his own way. He was about to be transformed to pass the seventh gate and had to pass the first door to walk through the gate, and he was waiting to be turned into a complete mortal. He went close to door number one, still in his invisible, celestial form. As soon as he set foot at the last door, he transformed into a visible body. At once, he started his quest and got busy going through the first door. First, he visited one of his best friends from the SOS team, to get some tips to cross in time. The SOS Lord informed him that he had to carry out this urgent meeting with care. He also explained to him that he had been chosen for a mission to Oxi, the perfect point Jus Supp had created. After a long conversation, the two friends left, and together they went to an earthly place to meet with their second and third SOS friends.

In their room, the three SOS amigos gathered for a long conversation. They grabbed onto three diamond-shaped beams to travel down to Earth Point.

Leerd took the red-yellow, and the three amigos took the blue beam, the yellow with two green lines. The seat designed in solid snow white was empty.

The solid, snow-white one remained empty; it was ready and reserved for the third SOS Lord who didn't travel, due to the warming of the planets and galaxies.

ZISHE'S ATTACKED

Joseph was curled up, hiding behind a big rock that shielded him; it was a wall for protection. He was watching out of Dr. Watters' entrance door. I was inside my room packing books, shoes, food provisions, and clothes that I'd take to Sun City for the last week of class. It was the last week of school because it was the end of the school year, and I was going to come back to Saint Nicholas Village for my three months vacation in a week. It was a Sunday afternoon; the sun was gleaming in the Pacific Ocean. Dr. Watters, as usual, was busy working in his candle-lit lab.

He's taking good care of his own business and not thinking about Zishe or me. Joseph, the Wizard kept looking for the right time to trespass into Zishe's room. Zishe was rocking herself in her chair and dozing off; she was sweating on the old, wooden chair; her garments were soaked. Joseph, the Wizard walked warily near the front door to take a closer look and plan the attack to murder her. And, after carefully checking out, and balancing the advantages and the risks he was facing, he went back to prattle to his soldiers who awaited his orders to be carried out and prepare for battle.

One of his three top hitmen spoke and asked him a question, "When are we dragging her and strangling her bony body, boss?" Joseph, the Wizard just shook his head and perched on a thick tree branch. They waited three more hours watching and calculating the movements to break into the property. They kept watching and looking at my room; the light in my room was still on. Joseph, the Wizard, and his army of infantry men were playing a weird, but fancy game. The game came to their twisted minds on the spot.

All of them paired up and started pushing each other only with the side of their heads, and the winner chose to shoot a single bullet at a target of an animal. The game went on for twenty-three minutes. When the game ended, they had a mountain of dead animals and broken branches on the ground. Finally, I turned off the light in my room and went to sleep, but Dr. Watters came in to flip the switch back on.

He had heard the gunshot and he was scared to death. He stood next to my window, watching the encampment of devil soldiers surrounding his house, ready to charge at us. Zishe kept vigilant, grasping her magic wand tightly in her hand. She knew Leerd would come to help at her call, but she was sure she couldn't beat Joseph, the Wizard with her human magic; she couldn't protect Dr. Watters, me, and herself with her magic powers.

Joseph, The Wizard called it off for the night. He dismissed his men and one by one they marched away in single file. Dr. Watters was still in my room, and we were watching the withdrawal of Joseph, the Wizard, and his army; I spotted Joseph, the Wizard at the end of the line; he was writing on a piece of red paper. He turned back and walked near my window and shot a single bullet that hit the right corner of the window frame. I ducked and dove underneath my bed. Zishe came out of her room and stormed into my room as fast as she could. She was worried about me because she thought I'd been hit and was probably already dead by now. She called me; she was roaring like a lioness protecting its only cub, but I was too nervous and afraid and not a single word came out of my quivering mouth. I tried to scream but every sound was muted; I took a lot of air in, to fill my lungs. A few valuable seconds had passed, and Zishe was about to faint; suddenly, she heard screaming coming from underneath my bed where I was curled up, and I popped my head up and crawled out.

Zishe and I moved next to the window. Joseph, the Wizard realized that I was watching him through a crack in the wooden window frame, but he didn't have any idea that Zishe was standing by my side, protecting me, and ready to attack him. He planned to give me an unforgettable show: first; he lay on the ground pretending he was dead. Zishe and I were checking him out.

Zishe knew we couldn't trust him, and that he was planning to trick us. In a second, we noticed Joseph, the Wizard turning into a colorful tropical red frog, then again, in a split second, he converted into a huge coral snake. The viper slithered at an unfathomable speed. It was coming toward the window. The reptile lurked up in the dark, on the wall, and hung upside down. The long snake stuck out its tongue, licking the thick bullet. Then, it swung away its head and charged to smash the wooden window frame. It repeated it a second time to spray venom on the wood to burn it almost halfway, in a second. I jumped back tripping and falling. Zishe watched me. Surely she'd seen enough; she stretched out her hand and aimed at the snake's head and shot a thunderbolt of toxic fumes from her wand, and the snake dropped into the bushes.

Immediately, the snake turned back into a human form. Joseph, the Wizard had severe burns and turned into a human inferno. He fled, holding one leg, and coughing and inhaling fumes He kept running, taking a shortcut, but suddenly, he was forced to stop; Thudil fired a thunderbolt missile behind his back, and blocked the narrow path Joseph, the Wizard was taking. The blast broke many tree branches and burned rocks reducing them to cinders.

Thudil showed up and confronted Joseph, the Wizard. He threatened him and forced him to fight back to the end or be sent to hell before his time. Thudil told him, "If you miss this opportunity to kill Mike Watters, I'll kill you myself!"

Joseph, the Wizard caved and pleaded his case at the same time; he said, "I had him, but that old lady attacked me; I'm sure she's an old Wiccan!"

Thudil interrupted him yelling, "I thought you were the king of the magus. But no way; you are nothing but a worthless magician. If you don't do the job right, I will send you to hell before your time is up, I repeat this as a warning!" Thudil's ghost became invisible once again, and Joseph, the Wizard sat to take a breath. He dozed off for a few minutes, then he woke up and headed home, alone because his army had already deserted him.

GOBBIT SOLDIERS

Many warriors with huge gobs on their right cheeks, were warding the premises and the dirt roads. I was getting back from Sun City to spend the entire summer vacation with Zishe. I was riding in an overloaded passenger bus. The sky was clear, and the sun was almost up in the middle of the sky; a single thick cloud formed in the sky and elongated for five miles, then, in a split second, plummeted and plopped loudly onto the roof of the bus. A pall of black smoke lowered down closer and started shooting bullets of fire mixed with rain drops of golden sulfur around the bus. It covered about a mile. The drops were so big, and they moved so fast that they made a few holes in the roof of the bus, and the water leaks were soaking all the passengers on the bus, except me. I was thinking about and watching the strange scene. I started to hear whistling voices.

The voices were clearly saying, "Don't go back for Zishe because she will be dead soon; Joseph, The Wizard was attacking her a few seconds back, and he's already butchered her; if you go he'll kill you too!"

I looked to the left, then to the right, I turned to look through the back of the bus and then looked straight ahead at the road through the smashed windshield. I discerned that the driver had been killed. All the passengers were dead, laying in a pool of blood and water. The bus was rolling by itself; I tried desperately to reach for the steering wheel to steer it and stop it from speeding and running away and falling over the cliff.

I was about to put my hands on the dusty, wet wheel to steer it, but a magic black carpet covered the windshield and blocked my visibility. I managed to sit, place my right foot on the brake, and slam the pedal. The bus turned over on its right and fell down a deep gorge. It rolled over bushes and rocks in its path, for about 900 feet and came to a complete halt in between two gigantic trees. I was soaked in sweat and blood. I opened my eyes.

Immediately, I closed them again because I didn't want to look down at the deep valley. I saw that the bus got caught by two tall pine trees that blocked it and avoided it from ending up in the shallow waters of Saint Nicholas River. I was trapped, hanging in mid-air. I kept thinking hard, but no productive thoughts came to my mind. My heart was pounding so hard, and my fists were thumping it violently; I assumed I was in that trap, like a rat caught by its snout; I knew that my heart would give in soon, and I'd have a massive heart attack. I called out for help and in a strange scream from the top of my lungs, I said, "Zishe, come, I need you!"

The wind blew hard, and it carried the message to her in a split second. Zishe received the message that I sent her urgently. She got in touch with Leerd, even though she knew he had been busy lately, solving important top-secret matters that Jus Supp had entrusted him with.

She posted on my message, that Leerd had responded to her, "I'll be there to rescue you and Mike, as soon as I finish this burden that's giving me a headache."

Then Zishe replied, "There's not much time left!" Leerd yelled, "Go now, or you will not be in time to save Mike!" Softly, Leerd replied a second time, "I will wait a few more seconds, so Thudil, and the whole universe will know that I have found favor in the sight of Jus Supp, from the very beginning of his creation, and I'm chosen, and I have chosen Mike to become MegAm according to Jus Supp's holy decree."

The strong wind that Joseph, the Wizard commanded to shake the bus, swept the dead bodies away so that all of them exited through the broken windows and dropped into the water and on the sharp rocks. Just in time, I grabbed onto a bar from a bent, sharp wedge of metal that was still attached to the floor of the bus. I looked at the corpses falling and landing in the basin, but I didn't give up hope.

The battered bus stopped rocking; I had silence and peace for a minute. I relaxed and took a breath. Bystanders were looking over the edge of the gully that was about five hundred feet away; some of them were enjoying the show Joseph, the Wizard was giving, and they kept cheering for him. Still, others were fearful to look Joseph, the Wizard right in the eye; they feared that they may be blown off the edge of the cliff.

He laughed and shouted these words at me, "The end of your life has come to you, boy! You know that Zishe, the old sorcerer is not a match for me anymore; she's too old, I'll beat her every time! And Thudil is stronger than Leerd for sure. I, Joseph, the Wizard," he added, "am sure darkness will defeat light in the end, and our world will rule and win for good. We will take over the universe, and I'll be the prince on this soon-to-be fully evil plane. Thudil has told me so!"

Then, Joseph, the Wizard stretched out his left arm and pointed to the bus, hanging and toppling over, and he shook it violently for half a minute; everybody saw my severely wounded body falling out the window. Most of the bystanders cheered for him and despised me, but a few of them supported me and burst into tears. My body was about to hit the ground; suddenly, a hand coming from heaven grabbed me, lifted, and saved me. Joseph, the Wizard saw this and fled instantly, and a second later I was on my way home, safe and sound. A couple of good people took care of me. They cleaned my wounds, disinfected my scratches, and covered me with plastic trash bags they found on the ground.

A cripple old man, missing an eye, ear, and leg spoke gracefully, "I have something to say, "Then he stuttered the following broken words, "I saw a golden beam of light, coming down from heaven, you know. It was falling vertically at a speed, you know; my eye followed it from the very top cliff, right there, you know. And I saw their feet before hitting the rocks on the uneven ground, and a rock split into four, opening four deep sinkholes. In a split second, one piece of the rock was magically turned into a scoop and caught Mike, then it arched up and made a U-turn, shooting him up to put him here for safety. And that's the truth, nothing but the truth, so help me Jus Supp!"

Delfee, a wannabe witch, and Joseph, The Wizard's childhood next-door neighbor, a well-known troublemaker, started interrupting. But, just then, a child yelled out, "Attention, everyone! A witch is talking! Open your ears and listen to the hag!" Delfee paused, then she said, "I saw what happened; ain't like the half-blind fella said. I saw my future boyfriend, Jack, the Wizard lifting his left hand; soon he lowered it and stretched it out. Immediately, he aimed it at the target. In the nick of time, he caught him in the net that he cast down a second before; he tied it with an invisible thick duvet on four strings so no stone would break his bones, in case he fell off the scoop and landed on the sharp rocks. So, there you have it! My suitor saved and spared the boy's life!" She was silent for a long time, then she continued her long speech, and ended with this phrase, "The rest is history."

The nude boy spoke again, "You're a liar, piece of crap, flat-butted, long-necked, toothless sorceress! You don't even remember his name, which is *Joseph*, the Wizard! You're a piece of dung, madam witch!"

ZISHE'S GONE

Zishe grabbed her powerful scepter and placed it in between her legs, over her wide-waisted skirt. She looked up and down for a second, then she started walking in circles, and then sat glued to her magic rocking chair. The air around her was very violent and deadly; a whistle was heard in the background, warbling every second. But she was alert, as she knew she was going to be attacked at any second; she got ready for battle. She stayed observant at all times, her eyes wide open, but at times, she blinked and closed them a little to moisten them to see better because she was very old, got tired easily, and felt weak. All parts of her body were old and slow to react. She knew I would come at any minute, and she was concerned for my safety. She was sure Thudil was plotting a mortal blitz to eliminate her, and he might take me prisoner, to get to her. She knew Joseph, the Wizard was watching her, day and night.

Joseph had told Thudil that his mission was outlined to banish me once and for all. Thudil screamed at Joseph, the Wizard that he mustn't fail this time. Thudil burst into a rage and sped up the blitz to gobble up and inject the venom into Zishe himself and with his own fangs.

Of course, Zishe knew she'd been waiting for the fatal blitz, so she was ready to hold her ground. She held tight to her staff all the time.

Suddenly, she heard the first shaft hitting the roof. Lethal smoke burst around the whole lot in a second.

She heard an evil voice again, that said almost whispering, "Mike has been killed. He's cold and dead; Joseph, the Wizard ended his life a couple of minutes ago in a suicide attack he planned, to assassinate Mike." Thudil was using a psychological tactic to distract Zishe; he knew that if she lost concentration and worried about me, he'd be able to win the battle and kill her once and for all.

Zishe heard that I was dead, and she started to cry blood in one eye and tears in the other. She opened her mouth wide, almost choking for eleven seconds, then she screamed, "No, not my Mike! Lord Jus Supp, save him! I trust in you, Lord, and my faith in you will never leave. I won't give up. I'll refuse to accept that he's dead unless I see his dead body with my own eyes, and you tell me, Lord Jus Supp, that you will allow my Mike to be with you cruising the galaxies today!" Zishe buried her face in her pale hands and wept.

Thudil quickly drifted so fast that he dropped three thunderbolts on the roof in a split second. The bolts opened up three holes in the middle of the house's floor. Thudil had a map in front of him showing Zishe's exact location at that moment. But, she cleverly hadn't moved at all in the last second that she'd checked my room. Suddenly, Thudil's choice was to storm my room to take my possessions, to convince Zishe that I was already dead.

Thudil started to celebrate the war that according to his reckoning, he had already won. The left wing of the house was already ablaze. Zishe knew she had to do something, right away; she didn't have many choices. She drizzled very fine magic drops over the flames. Thudil watched and noticed that the fire was going out; by now, he knew Zishe was still alive. Surely, he missed the target and Zishe was already giving him a tough fight. He rained a multitude of beams of fire, hail, and brimstone down onto the house. Zishe blocked all of them before they hit the roof; luckily, the thunderbolts exploding on the property didn't turn the house into cinders.

She was tired and couldn't keep her strength up much longer, and her arms felt too numb and weak to keep her wand up and shooting, and she couldn't stop toxic darts to defend herself and her property. And now she stopped thinking about me because her brain was pondering so hard whether to run or stay and fight. In that instant, all she wanted to do was save my room and protect Dr. Watters' lab from becoming debris and dirt. She cleared her mind to think. And forthwith, her brain came up with a brilliant plan that might just work.

Quickly, she jumped high up into the air through one of the holes in the roof that Thudil's beams of fire had made, and to make herself visible to Thudil in midair and outside the house because he was thirsty for her blood. Her idea was to flee into the fields and leave the house so Thudil could chase her and so she would save my room and Dr. Watters' lab. She knew she could be killed but that was her last and best choice. Thudil fell into the trap and started to chase her away to finish her up. And he was sure he'd send her to hell, according to his plans because he thought she was no match for fighting an open sword.

Zishe was about to land on her feet on top of the towering hill, standing majestically in the middle of a boundless valley, along the banks of Saint Nicholas River. When she was about thirty-three feet from the sword, she spun around in the center of a fake whirlwind that she created and directed her rod to point at her house in the distance. She sent thousands of pipes and hoses filled with fire extinguisher gases to put out the fire. Immediately, the flames stopped, and just a column of smoke moved up from the roof. High up, it formed a cone, sucked up everything in its path, including demons hanging out in the area, and burned out everything, expelling them out of the funnel's mouth.

Thudil who was tailgating her, turned around to see what was happening. He watched the houses still standing and looked at his army of evildoers dying. He went off the deep end and turned quickly to face and attack her. Thudil didn't realize that Zishe had already sent him a mortal torpedo. The deadly bullets hit him without giving him time to protect himself or to fire his most powerful invisible weapon.

Thudil bounced for about a mile, and landed on his devil butt, on a sharp cliff; he plunged nine hundred feet and ended up nailed to the peek of a long rock. He remained crucified to the stone for a few seconds. It gave Zishe a good amount of time to let up and prepare for the fearful attack coming from the angry Thudil; she expected it at any second.

Thudil got inside a tiny dark cloud of smoke; he was mad but full of energy, yearning to chew her alive, shooting rays of brimstone at her dead body and spreading her ashes in all directions. Just in time, she blocked the burning arrows and directed them back to the cloud where Thudil was sitting. He was attacked with his own ammunition, bringing him a self-directed counterattack.

Zishe saw me walking across the river, at a shallow and narrow spot up the stream, about, a mile from where she was fighting for her life. Thudil got back into action and took advantage when he saw her staring up the river, lost in thought. He launched an arsenal of thunderbolts, beams of sulfur, torpedoes of chemical burning hail, a whirlpool of dust, and fine sand to blind her, with all the dirt possible, commanding the wind to blow it into her tired eyes.

She put her rod close to her face and shook the magic stick to blow fresh air to clear her eyes, mouth, and nose to get rid of all the toxic fumes that she had been breathing in.

Zishe was tired, both physically and mentally; her brain was playing tricks on her body and mind, and her good feelings were leaving. Thudil was playing mind games with her, deadly tricks for her to surrender. She was about to give up the fight because she thought it better to die than to live one more minute without me. For she was sure she knew I was dead; the evidence was there. Thudil told Zishe that Joseph, the Wizard had killed me a few hours ago.

But she hoped and prayed the evidence, and the facts were wrong. Her hopes led her to believe she'd see me alive again in the future. These thoughts boosted her strength and brought energy to her physical body to keep on fighting to save her life. She was sure the battlefield didn't favor her to win the war against such a powerful enemy. She was lost in thought; she didn't know where she was, and she was not even aware that she had a plan B to beat Thudil. She turned her pleas to Leerd for help.

Leerd answered her in a second, He assured her that I was still alive. He sent her a message in a code to her sensory long-term memory. Leerd said, "Mike is on the way home, in fact, he's opening the front door this second. He's been worried about you. He's a fighter, he fought to the last second, and with a little bit of my help, he defeated Joseph, the Wizard! You should be proud of him, such a charming and handsome lad. There's no doubt in my mind the SOS angels chose him for the mission to save the children. Jus Supp chose him because he's the best to carry out this difficult task. Fight to the end Zishe, I'll protect Mike, but I'll let you win this fight all by yourself. It's a challenge, you'll win; I trust in you. I'll give you a hint," Leerd said, "Use plan B, the water current, and remember, the river will be your shield."

Zishe held onto the rod, jumped in the water, and started walking on the water, moving fast to the deepest pond in the river. She dove in, and she stayed underwater for a good minute and thirty-three seconds. She swam underwater in all directions, zigzagging. Thudil was shooting like crazy without a visible object or a target.

She stayed deep in the water for nearly a minute. She couldn't stay any longer because she was running out of oxygen. She needed to get out to catch a bit of fresh air, fill up her lungs and get oxygen to her brain. Thudil wasted no time, and aimed he thought, to shoot at her head; she ducked deeper, and the missile only splashed into the water, missing her.

Zishe stayed under without taking a single breath for a long time. Thudil kept watching her; he knew she would come up soon to take some air. On the other hand, Zishe was aware he was spying on her, and he'd shoot to kill as soon as she came out of the water, in fact, the very second she popped up her head. But she forced her brain to stay under the water. She ordered her brain to come up with a good plan to attack and not to slacken and stand her ground the very moment she chose to emerge out of the vital, sacred liquid.

SNAKES AND MERMAIDS

Zishe pursued her masterplan B; she was informed that Thudil wouldn't get into the river for two reasons: one, he was deadly sensitive to the water, and two, he couldn't float at all. So, Zishe had a trump card and all she needed to do was give it all she had. She assessed the situation briskly and came up with an astounding idea. She stroked her rod and grabbed it tightly, and started to make cool, weird movements with her long staff. She chose to touch a tiny fish with the tip of the rod; the tiny fish was turned into a gigantic mermaid; she also chose to touch all the shoals of fish swimming around her, transforming them into mermaids. She managed to give them a face and hair exactly like hers. All of them became Zishe's look-alike mermaids. It appeared it was her lucky day as she spotted thousands of snakes slithering on the riverbed and sticking their deadly tongues out to swallow guppies. Zishe wasted no time; she charmed them and then asked for a favor. The whole school of serpents moved their heads in acceptance of the request.

Zishe thought about her navy arsenal; she checked the computer in her brain, as a commander-in-chief makes the final check on the main computer of the submarine, before deploying the mortal computerized missile. She requested the first mermaid to go afloat to start the countdown to launch the challenger fleet, and she gave her a unique title, "Sacrificial Queen."

Zishe came out in smart military formation: The serpent soldiers made a circle wall, the Sacrificial Queen led the formation, and she held up a blue flag. She swam with elegance, adding a touch of sensuality to her strokes.

Thudil saw the heads bobbing up, opening up holes in the water; he shot the head of the first one that popped up and blew up her head. He celebrated his victory, thinking it had been Zishe, but the worst surprise was yet to come to his early celebration. Slowly, five more Zishe heads and faces branched out. Thudil looked at them and hesitated in shock for a moment, as he was not sure which one to eliminate first. He blew the head of the first, the second, and the third away, but two went back under the water and escaped.

Thudil was angry and afraid at the same time. He was trying to guess what kind of mind game Zishe was playing with him. Thudil was keeping his eyes closely on his opponent's next movements. Meanwhile, the snakes were busy assisting Zishe to carry out the essential details, to make sure the next plan would come to fruition, and to execute it to near perfection. The vipers formed a funnel, and the upper end went up ten feet above the water. The last snake became Zishe's eyes, a sort of telescope or a pair of binoculars. The telescope-eyed snake spotted a suspicious, weird guy running in the distance, and he was getting close to Thudil. Zishe implored the informer snake to keep her eyes open and her ears peeled to get me any valuable information. After the snake described the stranger to her, she was sure he was Joseph, the Wizard, who was encountering Thudil, and was up to no good, to inform the demons.

Thudil was busy watching the mermaids' and snakes' ruckus, so he didn't pay attention to what was going on behind his back. Joseph fell three times, and with every single one of his falls he managed to get up with at least three loud moans and continued going forward; his ultimate goal was to get to where Thudil was standing to notify him of the bad news that I had escaped and that I wasn't dead; he was repeating it in a loud voice. He was about thirty-five feet from Thudil when he fainted, and this time he couldn't get up, even though he was trying his best to get back on his feet. His stamina and strength gave up, and his mind and body stopped moving for about eleven long seconds. He screamed as loud as he could, but Thudil didn't hear any noises or voices.

Finally, Joseph, the Wizard woke up and said, "Mike's not dead!" Thudil turned and roared, spitting the loudest thunderbolt he had ever created; Zishe heard it while still submerged under the water. Dead birds that had been hovering along the river, dropped from the blue sky. The snakes dove back into the water to hide and protect their heads from being smashed by heavy objects and animals falling from the smog-filled sky.

Zishe was already informed because Joseph, the Wizard said to Thudil, "Mike's not dead!" Zishe overheard it under the water and gave a friendly, sweet, and heavenly smile to her new friends, the snakes, and the mermaids.

Sweetly, she told them, "Go back out, all of you, help me out. This time, I'll defeat him; it's my lucky day! Leerd, the only son of Jus Supp, and heir to the throne of the Maker and Creator of all in the vast universe heard my prayer. It is time to teach Thudil a lesson that obliterates his evil mind.

All the snakes swam up and stood on their tails, slithering around in a small group, forming a strong wall that no one would dare to climb. Hundreds of mermaids torpedoed to play a swimming game on top of the freshwater, on the right side of where Zishe swam. Thudil was in terror as he didn't know which one was Zishe. He was about to flee in desperation, but Zishe lit her rod, pointed it at him, and crippled him with the impact caused by the deadly, burning flames, and with the nuclear flaring gases; he looked defeated.

The fight was over for a short while. Zishe knew Thudil would stop at nothing but would come back stronger and angrier in the upcoming bout, for days and months to come.

Zishe and her new army of faithful amphibians swam against the wind and current, taking her up the stream to where the river starts at the foot of an arid mountain, called Round Peak. Soon, some natives spread rumors around that she had been carried by mermaids and snakes in a golden, seraphic craft. Other natives said she was taken by ethereal, transparent bodies with female faces, long blonde hair, and ten-foot-long snakes and fishtails, flying her ten feet above the waters, dressed in white robes.

Back at Saint Nicholas City, the gossiping and rumors about Zishe's whereabouts were spreading throughout the entire region. People standing on street corners started conversations such as the following: "Zishe was kidnapped by Joseph, the

Wizard; she was last seen fighting him and Thudil in the river valley, a few hours ago."

The inhabitants asked, "Will she return to her beloved city"?

Others answered, "No one knows!"

A blind old man, named Uncle Mat, stated that she was killed by the same ghost that had devoured Ed Tower's soul, some time back. No one knew the truth. Though the motive was known, not the truth. She was missed by all the people that dwelled in numerous neighboring boroughs around the green valley, and along Saint Nicholas River.

SCARY VISIONS

The first night that Zishe was swept away by the river current, according to false witnesses, she drowned, and her dead body was taken by strange mermaids. I kept processing it in my room, thinking for a long time; I went to check Dr. Watters' lab hoping to find him inside to have a chat with him to get some helpful answers to some of my questions.

Dr. Watters was nowhere in the house. I looked everywhere, but could not see him or find him, and my heartbeat slowed and almost stopped! I thought the worst had happened to him and was convinced that Dr. Watters got killed when Thudil bombed the house since half of the building had been reduced to dust and ashes. I went back to the lab a second time. I looked at the dusty table and spotted a glass with a little bit of wine left in it. I saw a note carefully folded inside, not touching the bottom of the glass. Carefully, I pulled it out and unfolded the wrinkled paper, and read it. I found out that Dr. Watters went to John Rudelir's place to visit a couple of patients that had fallen from a tall tree and were in critical condition.

Joseph, the Wizard came up with a new plan of action and changed his strategy, he wanted so badly to kill me. Now he tried to control my mind. He and his incubus started to come up every night with a way to play tricks on me, to freeze my brain, and to rape me, and all the other demons sent scary visions to torment and persecute me. These scary visions startled me as they were demonic. I was attacked in my sleep every night, and when I was awake, my physical body was slashed with invisible daggers; the brutal beating never stopped. And at dusk, as soon as the light was out, the dark images of incubus came floating in mid-air; shortly, the gigantic objects landed on my face and body, choking me.

I got trapped in a huge, dark urn and I couldn't even take a single breath because I choked under the heavyweight punches that crushed me. I couldn't even close my eyes because a long-tailed incubus jumped into my bed, terrorizing me. All I did was meditate and pray, hoping for a miracle from Leerd to send a luminary to help me. I thought of an angel descending from up high to save me, but help was not on the way, it was only a thought; I had to get the strength and stamina back to go through that scary night alone.

Joseph, the Wizard was watching me closely. Delfee remained posted outside the door, making sure, I was tormented every second of the night. She had an army of demons with bags of brimstone glued to their backs, to toss inside my room every hour. She forced the door every so often, to enter my room and throw the brimstones and put them back in their sacks every time they were running out of them. Some of the demons were blowing long whistle pipes dangling from their long, scraggly necks to blow them nonstop in my now almost-deaf ears.

They danced and celebrated, certainly they were throwing a wild demons-style party. They jumped and tramped on me, somehow managing to get inside my nostrils and mouth to try to throttle me to death.

Joseph, the Wizard's ghost came to me, stood next to my bed, and said, "You got caught, boy! There's no way out. Now, you're as good as dead! Soon, I will trap your mind. For the next two weeks, you're going to look at every object through four frames. And one by one, they will come to your face to crush it to pieces. It will go on the whole night, even when you turn the light on. The images will be scary, and torture you psychologically."

I tried to clear my mind, I rubbed and wiped my watery eyes, but the images kept falling and landing on my face. I wanted to run to escape, repeatedly closing, opening, and blinking my eyes. I couldn't rest and the trouble continued; I watched demons climbing up mountains, and some of them kept dropping and tossing rocks, breaking branches, and chewing dead animals' meat to show me their icky teeth. The smell was awful, the stinky odor spreading to every corner of my room. I was having trouble breathing since the fumes went into my eyes, my ears were growing deaf, and my mouth was numb; it was making it impossible for me to take a single breath of clean, pure air.

That dark night, from midnight to two in the morning, was a rough and tough one for me, I had been thrown into the furnace of hell to live with stinky demons having a devil's dancing party the whole night. Luckily, I lived through the night. and I fought the demons with meditation and prayers, the only resources I had available to win the first clash that Joseph, the Wizard had just begun with me that night.

MASTER BOJ

The next day, I walked along the river, fishing rod in hand. I stooped and in a couple of seconds, I sat down on the grass and looked up and down the river. I was still sobbing and devastated because I'd lost Zishe for good. I certainly thought I wouldn't see her again. I slowly stretched out my right hand, dropping the fishing rod. I lifted both hands and stood raising my chest; I saluted in honor of my beloved Zishe. A pool of tears fell from both eyes, and I waved her goodbye, thinking that I wouldn't be seeing her again.

An unknown ghost was watching me from a distance, riding a lightning-fast motor vehicle, which looked like a celestial motorcycle, with a steering wheel on both ends. The machine was an awesome, noiseless, and fancy piece of machine. The strange rider was dressed in a silver suit. His armor was galactic, and his uniform shone like the sun, indeed, it was as bright as the sun. He spoke to me in a special unknown code. He parked his vehicle and, got off it, and then he walked up to stand close to me and stood for a long time. He spoke softly in my ear and my mother language. He said, "I am here to teach you a code that Jus Supp wants you to learn before you become anointed by the three wise men, known as the Sons of Sun. You will be known as MegAm and you'll fight Thudil and the satanic Lucy

Fair van Ann who Thudil pick to drown all the children of the Oxi Terrain. And you'll be in charge of saving all people on Oxi, also known as Point Earth, or the Oxygen, or the Green Terrain.

"I am sure you know about this because you already met with them a few months ago. Then, you had a brief chat with them.

"Let's start the first class. Today's lesson will be just an introduction to the sound of the codes; you can take notes if you want. Anyhow, I am going to hand out a list at the end of the class.

"When you are in danger you just give the code for help, and I'll send you an invisible army of drones to protect you. I'm sorry, I forgot, I haven't introduced myself. How rude! My name's Boj, and I'm a billionaire, in fact, the richest man on the whole planet Oxi. I'm admired, respected, and loved by most people, that was the chief reason Jus Supp and his son, Leerd asked me to take care of you now that Zishe's gone. But, she will be back soon; she just took a short furlough from Leerd; don't worry about her. Oh! By the way, she's fine! She asked me to keep an eye on you and take care of you while she's away. As for Dr. Watters, he is having a good time at John Rudelir's place. He doesn't know about the troubles you and Zishe went through."

Boj turned around, went to his vehicle, and came back, then he assured me, "I solemnly swear, I will keep Joseph, the Wizard away from you; my army will keep a close watch on him. Every plot that he plans, I will know and stop him by any means available before he comes close to you. This is a short meeting. I shall say it's a brief introduction. I will meet you again soon, at least once a week to teach you all the necessary codes you need, to be ready for this special, but dangerous mission. Practice the ones I gave you. For now, go back home, and by the way, in a short time, Zishe will be back home to give you more details."

Boj waved goodbye, got on his fancy vehicle, and sped away. I stood still, waving him goodbye. I started my short journey back home. I ran fast because I was happy knowing that Zishe was alive, and I made it home in a few minutes, and without much trouble, opened the door and put away my fishing tools. The only problem I faced on the way back was an attack from a medium-sized, but ferocious snake that violently slithered to its hole after trying to penetrate its deadly fangs, to inject its deadly poison deep into my skin. Of course, it was a message sent from Joseph, the Wizard. A few feet ahead from the snake's retreat, I met with Delfee, Joseph, the Wizard's wannabe girlfriend. So, I knew, she was controlling and directing the viper to attack me.

On the other hand, I had walked the rest of the way, watching out for traps that might have been planted to snare me. Suddenly, a big net was dropped from a tall tree, I saw it coming down, and I ducked and dove just in time to get out of the way. I shook my head and breathed deeply to fill up my lungs with pure air.

A couple of minutes later, I left Dr. Watters' research laboratory, went into my bedroom, and to relax, I started to plunk the strings on the acoustic guitar, and sing my favorite tune; soon I slept like a baby.

JOSEPH RUDELIR'S EXECUTION

Dr. Watters examined the two patients lying in dirty cots. John Rudelir watched the doctor cleaning, disinfecting, and wrapping new bandages on his friends' wounds; they now seemed to be in stable condition. Joseph Rudelir, John's dad and a wealthy merchant, got up at 3:00 AM to saddle his fastest horse, to go on a long journey to sell his exorbitantly expensive cigar merchandise. He kissed his wife goodbye, and waved goodbye to his sons and daughters; they all gathered around to say a small prayer for blessings and a safe return. Joseph left, not knowing that he'd never make it back home again. He certainly wouldn't see his family anymore. Two of Joseph, the Wizard's butchers were waiting to cut his life short. Joseph, the Wizard planned to frame Dr. Watters and send him to jail for the rest of his life.

Joseph Rudelir directed his horse to the main gate to exit his property. In a few minutes, he got to the metal gate, got off the horse, walked to the lock, unlocked it, and pushed and put the key inside to open it. A few seconds passed, then he brought his three horses carrying the sacks filled with tobacco-dried and rolled leaves. He got back on his horse with the speed of lightning. But almost at the same time, a strong man wrapped his long muscular arms around his waist and his left hand took Joseph's expensive gun from the holster. They rode the horse together for eleven minutes. The man pointing the gun at the back of his head yelled to advance.

Joseph Rudelir didn't have a choice. He was unarmed and with the barrel of his own pistol pointed at the back of his head, he knew he'd be killed in a flash.

A guy called Lens, wearing thick glasses, was riding on the back of his horse, with the gun in his hand pointing at Joseph's brain all the time.

Joseph turned his head around and said, "Lens I thought you were my best friend. Why are you doing this?"

Lens laughed and said, "Money! It's a lot of cash, and dough means power, my friend!" Lens said, "Joseph, the Wizard is paying me. I'm going to kill you at the crossroad, and it took a lot of time to plan, but it'll take a few minutes to kill you, and frame Dr. Watters for murdering you; he'll be in prison for a long time, or maybe even a life sentence."

The horses moved slowly, tapping their hooves on the stones because it was still dark, and the path was narrow, stony, and uneven. It was winter, and it had been raining the whole night, the water was still running, and the mud was deep. They made it to the crossroads. Lens forced Joseph to go to the right. About 55 feet away was the perfect spot, with no rocks, mud, or water. Lens moved his gun to the right; he pulled the trigger and raised his right hand to shoot up in the air to warn his friends to attack Joseph Rudelir with machetes. He pushed him off the horse and his friend started to hit him with machetes and stab him with sharp blades.

Joseph Rudelir was dead in a matter of minutes; they cut off an arm and passed it to Lens, who tied it to the saddle pommel, threaded it to the horse's long mane, and sent the horse back home.

Dr. Watters was done about ten minutes before Joseph left. Despite John Rudelir's warnings, he headed home as he had been away from home for many days; he was worried about Zishe, since he spent the week taking care of John Rudelir's wounded friends.

Dr. Watters heard the din; it was a horse coming toward the Rudelir's estate at high speed. The animal sensed him, as Dr. Watters had ridden the horse several times before. He blocked the horse's way, and the horse stopped and lowered his neck; Dr. Watters grabbed the reins and patted his shoulders and ran his fingers through its long mane. The animal sadly neighed twice, then shook its head. Dr. Watters tried to guess what the horse was trying to tell him, but it was dark, and he didn't see Joseph Rudelir's arm hanging down the other side of the horse's neck.

Dr. Watters gave the animal the right to pass, the horse was slowed, hesitant to take a step forward because he was trying to warn him of the danger he'd face if he continued going in that direction. But Dr. Watters didn't understand and headed forward through the muddy path. The horse stopped after taking a few paces and neighed again calling Dr. Watters who didn't pay attention and kept walking as fast as he could. The horse moved further, and in a few minutes got to the gate and stopped to wait for someone to open the gate. Meanwhile, Dr. Watters was close to the crossroad, where he had to turn left to go down the hill to head to his home. Several feet before getting to the crossroads, his legs became numb, his hair stood up, and he tried to whistle a tune to calm his nerves, but his lips were so dry and tight that he was having a hard time even opening his mouth.

He knew something was not right, but he did not know that if he turned to the right, a few feet away lay his friend, Joseph Rudelir's dead body, cut into tiny pieces. Finally, he arrived at the crossroads; he stopped in the middle and turned to head to the right; he thought he wanted to go check it out, but his gut feeling warned him to go home at once. His skin still felt numb, and he rubbed his left arm with the back of his right hand, and he also felt goosebumps all over his skin. He walked down the hill so quickly, that he made it home in twenty-three minutes; it was a walk that usually took him fifty-five minutes.

When he was nearby, he looked at his house from the distance, stopped, shook his head, and couldn't believe what his eyes had seen at the crossroads; what an awful scene that was! Half of his house had been burned to the ground.

He ran fast through the gate, and saw a vision of Zishe's body inside, calcined and reduced to ashes. He came in and found out the main target had been Zishe's room. He was sure she was gone to eternity. He fell on his knees and led a short prayer by himself, and ended the prayer saying, "Rest in peace, dear Mom." He got up and went straight to his lab and saw that the note he had left a week ago was gone. This new finding gave him hope that, somehow, she had escaped and she was still alive. Dr. Watters heard a voice singing and the sound of a couple of strums of a guitar coming from my room. He went to check with a shovel in his hand to protect himself. He stopped by the door to make sure the area was clear and heard me singing; he sighed with relief and came in. I addressed him about what had happened and told him everything, even about the meeting I'd had with the wise man, named Boj, who had told me that Zishe was hiding somewhere, and she was still alive, and that she'd come back soon.

Back at the gate, Joseph Rudelir's horse was neighing and pacing back and forth along the large gate. Also, it'd been kicking the gate for the last hour and a half to get someone to open the gate for him to enter. Finally, John Rudelir went out to milk the cows, heard the horse neighing, and the noise when the metal was kicked and hit with its back hooves. He tossed the big scuttle into the air, and his mom and wife watched him running wildly to the gate. He was about to reach and touch the lock, but he halted when he saw the human arm hanging down from the horse's mane; he panicked and ran back inside the house. He left the horse outside, still kicking and neighing.

Ten minutes later John Rudelir and his mother walked toward the crossroads where Joseph's body lay, cut into pieces. They knew that Joseph Rudelir had told them the day before that he was going to start selling his expensive cigars at Pick Town, which was three miles away to the right of the crossroads. They went to the right and a few feet ahead they found the mutilated body lying across the narrow dirt road and blocking the pass.

Meanwhile, Delfee, the wannabe Joseph, the Wizard's girlfriend, and the almost-witch, had been pinned next to the gated property, where she was watching out to sneak inside the gate before it closed and to be an informer for Joseph, the Wizard, and to make sure his plot would be carried out to perfection.

As soon as John Rudelir and his mother left and before the fancy gate closed automatically, she went inside John Rudelirs house; a minute later, she entered the patients' room, and she choked both of them to death. She took the gauze, bandages, medicine, and other medical supplies Dr. Watters had left for his patients. She ran out and went through the fields, jumping and crawling through barb-wired fences and taking shortcuts to flee.

She ended up at the scene of the crime and hid in the bushes because John Rudelir and his mother were still sobbing.

Finally, John Rudelir spoke and said, "We need to go to Saint Nicholas to inform Dr. Watters; he'll tell us what to do." Delfee was listening and laughing as she was certain Joseph, the Wizard's plot was coming together just fine, and Dr. Watters would be behind bars soon.

All she needed to do was plant the evidence that proved that Dr. Watters brutally assassinated his best friend's dad. She had the evidence needed to convict Dr. Watters in her hands already, but she was missing an important matter, "THE MOTIVE!" She thought and thought hard to come up with a good motive. Delfee went back to John Rudelir's home and sneaked into John's room to do a quick search, then she went into his mom's bedroom, ripped a blank page from a dusty old notebook, and wrote, "Dr. Watters, I want to have sex with you because I think Joseph is having an affair with Rumula, your sister-in-law; payback, you know."

She searched through some important property documents to see her signature and fake it; when she found one spot where she had signed a living will, she laughed and said, "It was a piece of cake!"

She ran back to Joseph Rudelir's corpse and planted the evidence to frame Dr. Watters. She smeared stains of blood on a bandage, on the note, and a used syringe. she danced and dropped them in the middle of the crossroad.

The next day, Dr. Watters was arrested on first-degree murder; 'a savage and cruel assassination,' the judge printed in the first paragraph of his statement.

COURT BUILDING

Dr. Watters pleaded his innocence. His friends and most of the people of the land showed up to secure his innocence, and to demand the mayor and the police chief release Dr. Watters immediately. There had never been such a large protest in the 2,000-year history of Saint Nicholas Valley. Around 133,000 protestors, holding signs and chanting, "Release Dr. Watters," marched in front of the mayor's office and police building.

The police officers came out to end the peaceful strike by any means possible, according to the mayor and chief's orders. About three hundred officers and armed civilians brutally attacked the peaceful protesters and beat some of them up. The people refused to give in to the police officers' demands and kept marching, and the chanting grew even louder.

The officer started to tie the leaders of the protesters with thick ropes and dragged them to dark rooms. After they'd tortured them, all the leaders were beaten up; in a matter of minutes, John Rudelir called the army commander. The major and the police chief detained about three thousand protesters and piled them up in a three-room house next to the police station. The police brutality didn't stop peasants from supporting Dr. Watters; they kept demanding the police chief release Dr. Watters and leave him alone for good.

The commotion grew louder, and louder by the minute.

The local police couldn't manage to control the mob, but the mob had been marching quietly, and all they had been doing was exercising their God-given right to protest peacefully.

On the other hand, the mayor and the police chief had violated the people's rights and punished the poor peasants that had not committed a crime. They were abusing the law of the land, carrying out an abuse of power, rather than the rights of the people to protest. John Rudelir rode his best horse to Sun City to file as an alibi on behalf of Dr. Watters and a report for the police brutality complaint against the mayor and police chief of Saint Nicholas District.

The army commander and his pilot got onto the military chopper and took off from Base One Military Academy Point, and fifteen minutes later, the chopper was hovering over the protesters. He made his pilot land the helicopter on the colorful basketball court. The protesters escorted the general to the houses where the prisoners were kept. He ordered the police chief to open the doors, screamed at the police chief, called out to the mayor, and summoned them to an urgent meeting.

An hour later he handcuffed the mayor and the police chief and sent them to Sun City Military Prison in a military jeep. Dr. Watters was released immediately. He came out of his cell and walked tall through the square and all the protesters retreated carrying their beloved doctor on their shoulders.

Delfee and Joseph, the Wizard were in hiding on top of a hill watching how their plan was being ruined by the peasants. They got angry and set fire to the national forest and peasant straw huts, then disappeared through the thick bushes and shrubs.

I assumed that the legend was going to be written in all history books for future generations to read, that the peasants in the Saint Nicholas Valley's green region, joined a peaceful protest to free an innocent man from prison.

The police chief and the mayor appeared at the Sun City Military Court; they got a judgment of guilty and were sentenced to 15 years imprisonment.

Zishe showed up two days after Dr. Watters was released from Saint Nicholas District Jail. She told me how she fought Thudil to the end, and, in detail, she warned me to stay away from Delfee and to keep an eye on Joseph, the Wizard at all times.

Boj came to visit me and met with Zishe in private. They talked for a long time about my future training, to fight against evil, to defeat Thudil.

SUMMER VACATION

I took Betty out on a date for the first time. Giovanni Conde, my best friend, had given me tips to follow on my first date. I pulled out the piece of paper Conde wrote on with things to do and things not to do.

Conde jotted down, "The first thing you don't do on your first date is to ask your girl: Can you give me a kiss? Conde's advice, of course, was my personal piece of advice. And the first thing you do on your first date is kiss her on the lips, without asking. You got to gamble and take the chance; if she rejects you, so what!

I read the instructions quickly and put it back in my front pocket.

Betty and I were having a good time, holding hands and walking across the huge fairground parking lot. I stopped and looked at Betty straight in her eyes, she smiled, shaking and mumbling. I closed my eyes and kissed her on her lips. It was a gorgeous, sunny afternoon, and the weather was perfect, but when I opened my eyes after a long, tasty kiss, I saw a bunch of dark clouds descending, like shooting arrows from the blue sky. Rain fell in a matter of seconds.

Sadly, my date was put to rest before the real fun had begun. Delfee and Joseph, the Wizard were clapping and laughing, passing me a couple of times. They wanted to make sure I knew that they had caused the rain to spoil my first date ever!

A few blocks to the south of the fairgrounds, Moses, a kid that had hated me since elementary school, was riding his rusty old bike. Joseph, the Wizard spotted him and paid him to go and beat me up in front of Betty. Moses put me on the ground in no time with a shove, but Betty stepped in between Moses and me to stop him from jumping on me; he managed to pass her, and he threw the first punch at my face, hitting me hard.

I was bleeding, but Moses kept punching and jabbing me. Betty screamed, calling for help. I got up quickly and decided to fight back to protect myself, and punched Moses back with a heavy punch and I knocked him over. I rolled and threw myself down and landed on top of him, hitting Moses' face with my knuckles. I pinned him to the ground, raised my right fist, and then let it down with all my strength. My fist was about five inches from hitting and breaking his jaw when Betty yelled at me to stop. I barely heard her voice in the distance, so she grabbed me by my shoulders and pulled me away.

BOJ COMING BACK

I was trying to take a hasty nap; my head was spinning, and I couldn't concentrate at all. I was thinking about Zishe; my hopes of her coming back were dimmed; I was crying non-stop. I closed my eyes and prayed for a couple of minutes, asking for a quick nap. Leerd heard me and granted my wish. I dozed off for exactly two minutes. I woke up, with my guitar on my stomach, but I had no idea how it got on top of my belly. A sweet voice came down from the four corners of the ceiling.

I started to sing a song; I felt the presence of angels heard me singing alone. An invisible being grabbed my guitar from my belly and started strumming the last three strings on my guitar and sang along to the song. I heard the singing of a legion of heavenly angels, next to my ears. They memorized the melody, the rhythm, and the following lyrics of my song: "Tell me where you are. Why you left without a trace? Call me, oh call me, as the river passes by, I hear you in the morning, and as the sun sets in the sky." I interrupted them, just as I heard a soft rap on the back door. I stopped the party, as I feared for my life, and hid in a safe, narrow tunnel, Zishe had shown me a long time ago.

The deep hole was inside the concrete wall; I inched through it for a couple of minutes, hoping to get out of the house. I popped my head out, and immediately I felt a large, soft hand laid on my head. I screamed, knowing that I wouldn't see the light again. I was sure it was Joseph, the Wizard's hand grabbing me, and certain it was going to strangle me, or worse, chop my head off with one of his collections of silver knives. It took me a long time to open my eyes; the hand began to run his fingers through my hair and massage my skull gently.

I opened my eyes wide and looked up after hearing the man saying, "Come out, lad, I'll help you."

I was happy watching the familiar and unique face. It was Boj visiting me, to make sure I was safe.

Boj and I went out and took a long walk to rest in the woods; Boj did all the talking and I listened to all the warnings and advice he gave me.

Boj stopped on the side of the narrow, green sign, posted on the left corner of the dirt road. He placed his left hand on my shoulder and the right one he lay on my hand. He recited a few new codes and anointed me for the job that Jus Supp had chosen me. It had been assigned to Leerd to anoint me.

He kept saying the following: "About a year ago, you were walking by the big tree, remember?" I hesitated to give a proper answer, and a little confused, I nodded slowly. Boj continued: "The Sons of Sun met you that day, and talked to you about MegAm, the great superhero who will save the world near the end of time. And now, this time is around the corner, don't you agree? Leerd needed you to be ready because soon, the three wise men will return from the outskirts of the sun to put you in charge of this mission from Jus Supp. You have been chosen by Jus Supp himself to carry out the orders to beat the forces of Thudil, the destroyer of light and supporter of the forces of darkness."

Boj continued, "And, don't worry about Zishe, she's alive and soon you'll see her, as I told you last time we met. She wanted me to work with you, training you first. It is the will of Leerd to do it this way; we have no other possible course of action, lad. Leerd doesn't want Thudil to know where Zishe is at the moment; we need to keep him busy believing she's already dead. This way he won't harm you, and Joseph, the Wizard will wait because he's in trouble, and in hiding for the killing of Joseph Rudelir's charges. He had a perfect plan according to his evil strategy, to frame Dr. Watters for the death of Joseph Rudelir, but my people worked hard protesting to get Dr. Watters out of prison with the help of John Rudelir.

"One more thing, now, I want to give you this new information, and this comes from the very top leaders of light. But let's walk to the riverbank where we can be safe from anybody overhearing our conversation."

A minute later Boj spoke again, "Leerd wants me to upskill you in fighting, with unknown codes, but not with weapons. He also wants you to fight with your mind. You have to trust in yourself and have faith in Jus Supp, and yourself. And I promise, he'll fight all your enemies, and you will win big in every battle that comes along, and in the end, you'll win the last war.

"In time, I will upskill you in all the techniques and plans to develop your brain as nobody has done since the beginning, and no one will have a mind filled with military ground, air, and marine strategies, like yours."

MATILDA

I turned back time to reminisce about important information stored in my brain, I remembered the time when I was twelve years old. I was taking a seat on the big rock, which I usually sat on every time I walked that path when I went fishing. This time, I was grabbing my fishing rod, thinking of catching a lot of fish to celebrate Zishe's return; Dr. Watters had told me, she'd be back at 7:47 PM, from the longest trip she had ever taken, and leaving me alone for the longest time.

Dr. Watters was anxiously looking for a trustworthy caregiver to take care of me before he went on the trip. One day, early in the morning, Matilda was strolling by and offered to help him and assured him that she was going to take good care of me. And she also promised Dr. Watters, she'd lay down her own life to ensure my safety. So, Dr. Watters had gone to Sun City about three hours earlier.

I sneaked out to go fishing, without asking for consent from Matilda. In the meanwhile, three days earlier, Dr. Watters had met Zishe at a neighboring town, and taken her along as she needed to buy clothing and toiletries, and some antique jewelry she liked to get every once in a while. She usually took this special trip once a year, during the hot and sunny season.

Matilda said they were walking in the narrow, tarred streets on the outskirts of the city, toward downtown. Ten minutes later, they were walking on cobblestone streets, in the heart of the city, where all the good shops were located.

I had spent a couple of hours fishing, and my eyes were weary and watery, but I hadn't caught anything yet. I took a deep breath and passed out in a minute. I raised my face, and opened my eyes wide; a small, round shadow was rising above my head. The dark point stopped in the air for a few seconds; I rubbed my eyes to clean them and take a better look. I stared at the dot, and slowly the dot came down and fell on the tip of the fishing rod and cut the string. I stood up and quickly tried to run to find a place to camouflage myself, but a strange man was blocking my path. He shook his head and put his dirty hand on my shoulder. He laughed and pushed me back down to the big rock. I was afraid, as this was the first time I'd seen Joseph, the Wizard.

Talking quickly, the strange man introduced himself, "I am Joseph Cis, also known as Joseph, the Wizard, and I am the Son of Bernard Cis, the famous Magician, and founder of 'Bernard University.' My dad was a good friend of Dr. Watters,' your dad. In fact, my dad spent a lot of time recruiting him to join and enroll and take courses, but he refused. Doctor Watters is a foolish man, a dude with his brain who would have been a perfect fit to serve our Lord Thudil and the forces of darkness, and Thudlil is the founder and sole ruler of darkness.

"You want to know what Dr. Watters' problem is? He's too honest and is a weak and soft-hearted man. You, on the other hand, are different; I hope, you think about it a little and I urge you to join our team. You'll have all the precious commodities that money and power can buy if you join the devil's den of cohorts. There is something unknown to you; you don't even know me at the moment, but you'll find out in a short time. Certainly, I will ask my Lord Thudil to be stoically accepting of you. I'm sure he'll love to have you in his army, and that's the truth because we are liars. And, by the way, Matilda, your babysitter, is my only sister, and she let you escape for me to meet you, so I can chat with you. I know it's strange to you, but everything has been planned by me.

"Don't fret! If you think about it and join us, everything will be cool, but if you refuse my offer, I'll make sure you go to hell for the rest of your life. Don't be foolish like your dad; make it happen for you. If you join, that will be a punishment to Dr. Watters for refusing my father's offer. But, in case you do as Dr. Watters did, I'll stab him in the heart, making your heart miserable!"

Joseph, the Wizard made his last request, and added, "Make up your mind, the sooner the better!"

I watched Joseph, the Wizard as he disappeared into the green shrubs. He picked up the broken fishing rod, and I looked sadly at the spot where the line had sunk a few minutes ago.

BERNARD UNIVERSITY

The story of crowning Joseph, the Wizard, the king of the wizards, happened twenty-three years back, way back before I was born.

Bernard took a stroll at midnight along Saint Nicholas River, he was talking to himself, trying to put his evil thoughts together. He thought out a plan to recruit many children in the vast green valley; he walked around huts and dirty mud roads to ask peasants to join in the devil-worshiping school that he was founding.

He had set his sights on his sons: The first choice was Joseph who would be known as Joseph, the Wizard, then Pillar, the Hitman, Igus, the Thief, and Minggus, the Magician, and his daughter Matilda, the Informer. He also discovered the great talent of her younger daughter, Josephine, the Fibber, and he chose her to enroll in the School of Lies, and that's how she became known as Josephine, the Liar.

Bernard heard a cry and a demonic roar calling him; he stopped to watch the movement of Thudil. Suddenly, a ghost landed and planted its feet in front of him, blocking his path. The spirit of destruction took him to a cliff that in the distant future became known as the Tower's cliff, way before the savage sacrifice of Ed Tower, led by Joseph, the Wizard."

The voice told Bernard: "Thudil said, your son Joseph, the Wizard, will sacrifice a man here on this cliff; it will be a satanic ritual to honor the contract signed this very moment by you and me." Thudil ended with, "I set the rules of conduct to follow and control the valley, and one day we will rule the entire Saint Nicholas Vally."

Thudil commanded Bernard, that his son Joseph, the Wizard, must present an offering of a human on the cliff, the orders and regulations are signed in a pact of a human sacrifice that will be offered to Thudil, the Devil who himself will pick the soul in the future. That night Thudil gave Bernard three special evil orders and tools: A bandana with the inscription, Shadow Worshiping University, written on the ribbon. He also received a demons' worship book to pass to all students. And a magic word carved on a human rotten, stinky bone hanging around his neck and he was to always wear it, as Thudil's obedience insignia.

The ghost tied the bandana around Bernard's forehead; from that moment, he was ordered to never take it off, not even when asleep because that was the alliance, so he wore it till the day he died. So, that was the pact between Bernard and the Lord of Darkness, to sacrifice a human soul on the edge of the cliff, to quench the devil's thirst for human blood so Joseph, the Wizard would grow up and carry out the sacrificial mission.

Then, Thudil told Bernard to force Constantine Watters' son, if needed, to make him enroll at the Shadow Worshiping

University, and to recruit him while he was a little boy, to join, and enroll at Bernard University, as soon as possible. Bernard kept walking, and the demon ghost rolled his eyes and turned them into two popping balls of fire. He fired flames that hit the ground eleven feet away from Bernard; it was a sign to stop right there. Bernard froze, waiting for new directions from his demon chief.

The ghost jumped down the cliff, then came up, and set foot next to Bernard; he hurled blazes with his left eye and carved letters on a huge rock, then he fired with his right eye, and cut a thin tablet with writing etched on it. He blew fresh air with his nostrils to cool down the piece of stone, handed it over to Bernard, and flew away. Bernard put it in his satchel and didn't bother to read it because it was too dark, and he couldn't see a single thing.

Bernard arrived at his den within thirty-three minutes; the clock hanging on the rod of a curved post read 2:11 AM; he lit a candlestick to read the message written by the ghost fingers, on a rough stone tablet. He didn't know how to read very well, so it took him a long time to read the two lines. After reading the inscription he shook his head and went to sleep.

CONSTANTINE WATTERS

Joseph, the Wizard was just a teen when his father, Bernard enrolled him at Bernard University to learn the witchcraft trade.

The day before, Thudil had informed Bernard to force Walter Watters to sign a wizard deal with the devil. But if Watters refused to comply, he ordered Bernard to threaten and gaslight him, day and night, for refusing. Bernard died a few weeks later. But he had already taught his younger student, and son, Joseph, the Wizard to kill Constantine Walter's son, Walter Watters if he didn't join the shadow spirit group.

Before he died, he also sent his brother, Rosent, to tutor Joseph, the Wizard, and to take care of him because he was a minor. When Joseph, the Wizard turned seventeen, he chose his cousin, Nila, an honest and good-hearted lass to deceive Walter Watters and make him believe she was in love with him. Soon after Dr. Watters met Nila, I was born; my father being Dr. Watters, and my mother, Nila. And this is how the story of the fake burial began.

Joseph, the Wizard planned a fake burial to create the legend of Saint Nicholas' Angel. The story went like this: Walter and Nila had a baby boy, named Mike Watters. Joseph, the Wizard, and

Nila planned to sacrifice the baby to please Thudil, by killing the baby inside a casket, and the baby's heart was supposed to be eaten by my mother. Of course, that baby was me. A week later, Joseph, the Wizard started his evil plan to offer my soul to Thudil.

General Constantine was Walter Watters' father; he was a tough military general, but a loving and caring father. He took good care of his beloved wife, Zishe, and her three sons, James, the firstborn, who was a slow learner, Walter, the middle boy, whom Constantine trusted, and had a bunch of high hopes that he'll become a good military man because he was smart and dedicated to his work, and Walter had a great, athletic body. General Constantine enrolled him in the most prestigious B Hall Military Academy, but Zishe disapproved of it, so, he just attended one semester at the B Hall Military Academy. And his younger son's name was Patrick, who died at three from liver complications, after minor surgery.

Bernard's sights were set on swaying Walter to become a wizard, and inspiring him to sorcery, and he spent a lot of time every week brainwashing him. In fact, one day, he brought him a special witchcraft book, called 'Infernal Adoration.' He showed him magicians' demonic tricks. He begged him to attend his Shadow Worship University for a free class, but the boy always found a way to say no, without irritating the old wizard because he knew that he might hurt him if he told him no straightaway.

Bernard spied on the boy, day and night when Constantine wasn't around to protect him. He hired his brother, Rosent, an expert thief, to kill General Constantine so he could freely do the dirty job of persuading Walter.

General Constantine, as usual, unexpectedly came to check on his family, and to make sure that everything was running smoothly with his boys, every so often. One night, he came for a brisk visit, and when he was a block away from his house, he saw a man standing in front of the window, peeking into his house. He was looking straight at his wife's room. Constantine got close to the suspect who didn't pay attention to what was going on around him, and the suspicious observer got caught. General Constantine came up behind him on his tiptoes and grabbed Rosent by his neck.

He gripped it with his big hand and long fingers, and whispered to him, "What the hell are you doing spying on my family?" He removed his right hand from his neck, pulled out his concealed gun, and placed the tip of the barrel to his temple. Still whispering he said, "You are going to die if you don't talk!" He was shouting, "NOW!!" Rosent groveling, mumbled the words, "Cousin Bernard sent me; he wants to turn your son, Walter, into a wizard." General Constantine released him, telling him, "Get the hell out of here!"

From then on, Rosent's hatred became personal, and he swore to himself to take revenge. Rosent and Bernard became angry and together they plotted to kill him. And Rosent swore he was going to kill General Constantine with his own hands.

Rosent's plan of action and threats to assassinate General Constantine Watters never stopped, and he gaslighted him for the rest of Rosen's life. By the way, seventeen years later, Rosent was executed by a firing squad after he was found guilty of stealing a yoke of oxen. But, before he died, he followed, and attacked General Constantine every time he came to Saint Nicholas Village to visit his family.

General Constantine used to travel once a week from Sun City Military Station to bring groceries, clothing, and first aid medications to his wife and children. Rosent had assigned informers to watch the main roads and inform him when General Constantine was near the town of Philtekea. He hired a bunch of hitmen to ambush and attack General Constantine before he reached his destination at Saint Nicholas Town. Philtekea was a mile from Saint Nicholas Village. The road was hilly, and rocky, with a deep gorge, and a muddy gutter which was the main concern of travelers.

General Constantine usually trekked this dangerous territory by himself, and at night. Rosent's army of criminals used to hide at the end of the gorge, throwing small rocks several yards ahead of his horse, and a few of them every three minutes to the back and front of his black Mustang stallion. They just wanted to scare him, and to let him know that he was being watched, as those were Rosent's orders.

General Constantine was a man full of insight, and he was aware that they would not harm him; he also knew it was a warning sent from his worst foe. He always kept his rhythm, holding the reins with his left hand and his gun drawn in his right hand, his index finger touching the trigger and ready to shoot if necessary.

Rosent's boys didn't dare to attack for two main reasons: First, his boss had hired them just to follow him to observe and report back. They were not authorized to kill him, even if their lives were on the line, in other words, even if it was a matter of life and death. Rosent had reserved the right to torture Constantine and kill him with a single shot to the heart, and, with a silver poisoned arrow. This was a promise he had made to the army of demons that he served.

Second, General Constantine was the fastest drawer in the country. The army had given him the first Golden Medal of Honor, the first ever given to a member of the army. General Constantine had arrested the top ten criminals that had plagued the country for the last thirty years. And the bunch of gangsters knew they would never take him down, so, they kept from getting too close to him. And they never tried or dared anything stupid for those last ten years, except just gaslighting him.

THE ARMY SWEEPS
THE SWAMP

General Constantine was assigned a warrant to arrest Igus, the Thief, who had been terrorizing the people for many years. The army drove from Sun City at 11:00 PM and made it to Igus' hut at about 2:00 AM. They called General Constantine to march out and circle the home since the chopper was already hovering over the house; they were given seven minutes to barricade Igus' den of thieves.

General Constantine's chopper left to lead the military assault by air and kept him pinned to the house's front and back entrances to the house. He knew that Igus had a lot of connections with the military's high-ranking personnel and the local police department. Three months back, a military mission was scheduled to arrest him, but Igus had left five minutes before the armed soldiers arrived. A collaborator had notified him to leave his den that night because a search warrant had been issued to arrest him. But that night was different, and he tried to escape the rain of bullets piercing his body.

ROSSENT'S AMBUSH: Rossent had been notified that General Constantine had come to Saint Nicholas Town, and the next morning he was going to have a mandatory assembly with the mayor, in the city hall. The town hall was located in Tlam City, about two miles from Saint Nicholas Town.

Rossent planned to bring about his ambush to get rid of General Constantine, ahead of time. H climbed on top of a tall crag. General Constantine was walking six hundred feet away. A minute later, General Constantine was strolling next to the rock on an extremely narrow and dangerous path. Rosent dropped a huge rock on his head to flatten General Constantine. General Constantine ducked, rolled, drew his gun, and opened fire. Rossent jumped off the crag and fled at once.

BERNARD'S LAST MEETING: Twenty-three years had gone by since Bernard got shot in the stomach; he had planned a holdup that when wrong. It was a big criminal organization in which Bernard was training with his sons, and this activity failed. Bernard was severely wounded with a single gut shot.

He had taken his three young sons for training as he hoped to hit the jackpot. It was the first assault he was facing; he thought it was going to be easy, sort of like a practice run with the boys. But he had picked the wrong magnate. Joseph Waal was one of the richest and most powerful men in the valley. Bernard surrounded Joseph Waal's residence, as he'd planned to murder him and take all the money. The magnate had a huge net worth; there were rumors among the natives that he had seven large sacks filled with large bills, all cash. They were going for the jackpot, estimated at 10 million dollars. Igus opened fire ahead of time, and this cost Bernard his life. Joseph Wall fired back, and a poisoned slug went through Bernard's stomach.

THUDIL'S REAL NAME: Bernard was dying; he had only 33 hours to live. Thudil came to his death bed to tell him that his name was not Thudil. He called himself the Beamhell, the one who came from hellfire to get souls to burn in hell every second. He had used the name Thudil to trick people because Thudil was the voice of the Supreme Justice of the land, the Creator of Goodness.

The devil argued with Bernard that he didn't do his job well because he couldn't get Dr. Walter Watters to join his army of human blood drinkers.

Bernard knew that he was in his last days, and Thudil still pressed him to go get Walter and made him sign at Bernard University before he died. Thudil revealed his name to Bernard at the last second of his life, so he didn't have time to share it.

ROSSENT EXECUTED: A month after Rosent attacked General Constantine from the top of the crag, he was charged, and convicted of robbery. One morning a small jet hovered around the high peaks over the mountain range, trying to find a spot to make an emergency landing.

The pilot tried to land the broken iron bird on a long, muddy cattle field. The pilot was lucky to find a heap of cattle manure and a pile of dry hay that stopped the plane from crashing on the big rocks.

This event brought the army to investigate, and the police to report that the jet and the pilot were from a neighboring country. They made a stunning discovery. By chance, evidence was found to charge Rossent. He was found guilty of stealing and executed by a firing squad the next day.

SLITHERING

Constantine was riding his horse at about 7:33 PM, coming from Sun City; he had been strolling on the route for three hours. He was tired and thirsty, and an old beat-up car passed him and blew dust, blinding him for a few seconds. He wiped off the mud and dust from his face. He had just crossed the mountain range coming from Sun City, and he was galloping along the vast Saint Nicholas Valley, about 45 minutes from his final destination in Saint Nicholas town. His wife, Zishe, and children didn't know he was coming because he wanted to surprise them, as he often did. He probably wanted to catch them off guard.

He got off his horse to rest and tied it to a fence post. He walked to wash his face in Saint Nicholas River which ran along the muddy dirt road. He was taking his time, minding his own business when suddenly, the earth started to shake; he raised his head, and spotted an unnatural phenomenon; a large, dried gutter was turning into a river, and connecting with the Saint Nicholas River, on the opposite side from where he was standing. The ditch originated from the foot of the mountain, and a dark sinkhole was shooting up muddy water. He peeled his eyes to a gigantic, fifty-three-foot-long serpent slithering in the canal. The reptile was around three feet thick. General Constantine jumped on his horse and sped nonstop the rest of the way. Luckily, he made it home alive.

DOCTOR SAINT BARRIL

Going back to the last day Bernard Cis was still alive, Thudil gave the order to the demons not to put Bernard to death too soon. Thudil, the creature, sent demons to torture Bernard nonstop for 666 seconds and left him to pray for the last hour of his life. Bernard started to panic and tried to undo the deal that he had signed with the master of tricks and lies. His sons and daughters sent for the corrupt Dr.Saint Barril, the evilest doctor in the province, and the whole region of Sun City District. Dr. Saint Barril was hired to put Bernard to death by lethal injection. But when Dr. Saint Barrel came in, Bernard was already dead.

Evil Joseph, the Wizard was waiting for me at the banks of the Saint Nicholas River a few days after Bernard died. I was not there, as he was swimming at the large pond waiting and chuckling. He'd been waiting every day to learn more about me, but for the last three weeks, I hadn't come fishing, because Dr. Watters banned me from going near the banks of the river for an unknown period.

When he found out that I had been watched, he said, "This time you'll be locked up in the house; it is necessary, to avoid a possibly fatal attack from Joseph, the Wizard; you know he'll do anything if Thudil, the spirit of evil asks him to hurt you, he'll even end your life with a single shot. Remember, he's young and evil!"

FIVE TUNNELS: Thudil grabbed Bernard's body; he collected dust from the ground and wet it with tears, and he molded the clay and made a long flat rock; he put Bernard on top, so the small stone looked like a submarine. He looked toward the surface of the water and tossed it. The object floated five feet under the water and split into five little pebbles, and each one went a different way. After they floated to the end, they came back and stuck together, becoming one again.

BERNARD'S SCHOOL MISSION

Thudil asked Bernard before he died, to found the school that he called "Submarinology." He enrolled only one student, Martin Rivers, before he died, to teach him how to build under the sea. He was one of the three brightest minds of all time. He became an expert aquatic engineer. Years later, he was the chief engineer, building five secret tunnels under the sea. His mission was to build five tunnels to connect every corner of planet earth for Thudil to move his warfare arsenal.

THE TAIL

Dr. Watter and Zishe knew I was going to try to dupe them, so they locked me in to keep me from going fishing. I couldn't stop thinking of catching fresh fish for Zishe. It had been thirty days that I'd not gone out, in fact, I hadn't seen or gotten any sun for that long.

I was a teenager, and my brain wasn't sharp at all, so I planned a fancy escape, but I could not come up with a brilliant plan. I thought for a second, and I drew maps on the wall, notebooks, bricks, and other objects. In the end, wracking my brain with worthless thoughts, I gave up on all my ideas and choices and rested for a long time. One night, I heard someone scratching, knocking, and pounding inside the solid concrete wall. My mind couldn't envisage that that was the way out to freedom.

The noises were repeated seven more times every day, for three consecutive days. I got very scared; I was sure Joseph, the Wizard was opening a hole in the wall to get in to kill me. I could even see with my mind's eye, his particular weird, fancy attire; to me, it was the unique and special choice of weapons hanging from and attached to his whole body.

Zishe gave me eggs for breakfast, I mean every single morning, quail meat for lunch, exactly at noon, and fruit salads for dinner, usually at 6:33.

I placed the leftovers on the floor beside my bed, and I flushed the bathroom toilet. Strangely, after three days the strange noises inside the wall had stopped. One morning, I lifted my head to look at the wall, and I stared at the leftovers that somehow had moved five feet up from the floor. I turned to the door, looking for a way to escape. I turned back to the wall and saw that the food was gone, but someone had dug a large hole; I noted it was big enough for me to fit in it and get out to have some fun. But first I asked myself, who could have eaten the leftovers? It was a mystery! Despite that, I proceeded, but I still needed an answer to my question.

I checked a set of marks that I found: I glimpsed one single, long animal hair, and many paw prints. I set an investigation plan into action to find out about the prowler that was stealing my food. After hours of hard work, I solved the puzzle and came up with a hypothesis. The fellow was four-legged and came out of the toilet, but it wasn't an animal nor a human being, but both. I went to sleep late that night because I wanted to see the visitor with my own eyes, to make sure my life was not on the line.

Before I went to bed, I set an animal trap next to the food under the bed. Soon, I fell asleep, and I woke up early the next morning and got up in a hurry, but to my surprise, nothing worked in my favor; there was nothing caught in the trap, but the food had been eaten. The clever visitor moved wisely past the snare and licked the last crumb of bread and meat he could find on the floor!

I set the trap the following night again but made a few clever adjustments that could only be undone by another human being. It will be impossible for an animal to be that intelligent, to move the trap and free itself. I did not dither for a second to set my mind thinking and to reasoning wisely.

That night I went to bed with high hopes of seizing the intruder. Soon, I was snoring because within eleven minutes I was out for the night. The next morning, I raised my head to look from the bed to the floor, and I saw that all the food was gone again, but the trap was empty. Head down, I got up so fast, jumped on my feet, and tiptoed to take a closer look at the trap.

I said, "A tail? What sort of joke is this that Joseph, the Wizard is putting into my mind to poison it with lies?" I budged the trap with the tail glued to it and measured it with a shoelace. It measured thirty-tree inches long, and it was half an inch thick.

I picked it up and put it in a thick metal box. I put the palm of my hand under my chin, and my elbow on my lap to push up on. Suddenly, I said in a loud voice, yelling at the top of my lungs, "I was silly! All I had to do was call the plumber to dig deep in the sewer pipes to catch the pipe-human" I went through reading several old, greasy, puzzle-solving books, then I set my eyes on a dusty magazine I saw in the corner. I picked it up and flipped the pages a couple of times, but I found no plumber.

I pored over a page from the last pages of the magazine and found a name circled with blood, and read the following insert: 'George, the Wannabe Plumber.' I read it out loud, and a mystical demon plumber showed up with wrenches, a red plumber suit, and with a cut, bleeding tail. George the Wannabe Plumber immediately went to work, and in a matter of seconds, he had done away with the toilet and pulled out a gigantic, dying rat. Magically, the diameter of the pipes were too narrow for a fat human body sliding through it, but George managed to slither into the pipes.

A sweet voice told me that that was the way to go out and get fresh air, and to take a moment to go fishing. I listened to the voice and followed the instructions that were sent through my head. I went into the hole, head-first; nervously, I clambered into the dark pipe, and a couple of minutes later, I was far away from my cave, and there was no way back.

Then I realized, I had perhaps made the worst mistake of my life; I had disobeyed Dr. Watters. Demons were singing, and cheering!

A goblin demon spoke loudly, and said, "Let's give our guest, Mike, a breather."

A choir of huge fat demons sang, "Mike deserves it." A mouse and a large rat were featured on a large screen. George, the plumber's face popped up, he was the screen anchor. He gave a long speech telling me that Joseph, the Wizard had marshaled me to escape and go fishing, and, that Dr. Watters wouldn't dare to rescue me because Joseph, the Wizard planned to bring me back in a few hours after I had a good catch of Sunfish, the ones Zishe loved to taste the most.

Another green creature flying over his head announced that Joseph, the Wizard planned to keep me locked up forever in the Bone Devil Well. He added, "It was a rat, and it was George, The Wannabe Plumber that made it possible to plan your escape, and from now on you'll be our guest of honor. You should get used to staying alive among us, and revere Thudil, the beast, as we all call him among ourselves."

I slid and crawled quickly into a silver pipe that I saw hooked to the main rusted tube. The entrance was closed by an unknown force by just a hair's breadth before a gigantic demon grabbed my left foot. Instantly, the pipe was sealed with a white foam mist, and air conditioning was blown to give me oxygen and fresh air to breathe without pain, inside the narrow rusty tube.

But Leerd came to rescue me, and he had built a silver chute filled with water vapor to funnel me out of the filthy drains where Joseph, the Wizard's dark angels had me to be roasted in the devils' soul-baking furnace.

In a split second, I was gently vomited out into a green pond under a fancy tent. I was free and back to safety.

I opened my eyes and found myself about 300 yards away from my usual fishing spot. I walked slowly and went to sit on my favorite rock. I dug under the rock and pulled out a dirty fishing hook with a folded string that I had hidden three months ago; I moved toward a dried bamboo bush and cut a long branch and made it into a long stick to tie the cord to.

Back at the sewer, Joseph, the Wizard had a terrifying fight with the demon. He was beating them up; the punishment was severe, and each soldier was receiving one-hundred and eleven fireballs to eat and the balls were exploding, one every minute. Each explosion was tearing their bodies to pieces. The agonizing moaning and screaming were making the whole planet shake, causing a major quake, such that the demons had never felt.

Joseph, the Wizard was torturing the huge soldier to his right, and on his left, the dwarf one. He was asking them over and over again where the rat's tail was that I had hidden in my room. He needed to get hold of it because it was the scanning system he used to gaslight and find me. He had sent his army to all the drainpipes and tubes around the town searching for me but he could not find the tail, because Leerd had been following his sinister criminal activities, and he kept tracking him to cut short his plans to get to me. He had sent me the box to safeguard and lock the wizardry tail for eternity. The tail's powers were harmless as long as no one opened the chest and set it free.

The devils kept the search going by swimming in poo to please their angry boss, who was demanding they find the tail in a hurry. Meanwhile, I was happily fishing and wasn't aware that I was in danger. I had been fishing for fifty-five minutes and I had caught nothing.

A spy saw me from a distance and alerted Joseph, the Wizard. In a flash, he got on the move and was a few yards from me to pick me up.

DOUBLE CATCH

I was minding my own business and only thinking about fish, fish, and fish! I stood up for a second and cupped my hands over my eyes to see clearly, for the sun was blocking my vision. I stretched out and lowered my knees back to rest them on the smooth rock and sat on the crest of the rock. I returned to my fishing strategies. I closed my eyes for a few seconds and began thinking that I needed to catch at least one fish to bring to Zishe. I also put my ideas together for Dr. Watters, to justify why I had left the room without his authorization.

I came up with an idea that would clear up the whole mess that I had gotten into; I thought it was a good alibi. I thought that I had to tell Dr. Watters and Zishe the truth, as I couldn't and wouldn't lie to them, so help me Leerd, son of Jus Supp. I said to myself, telling the truth is life, peace, and... bliss.

I dropped the hook in the deepest waters and lingered for a long time, but no fish came around the hook for a bite. A good fifteen minutes slipped by before I pulled out the line to check the hook and changed the bait for a fresh worm. Shocked, I saw the hook never had bait the whole time I'd been fishing! I got mad at myself, got up, and kicking rocks, I walked away angrily. In one of my kicks, I turned a rock over, and a snake popped out; it sat on its tail, its head high up ready to strike me. I bobbed out of reach of the reptile and landed on muddy sand and stones that had rolled everywhere.

But my luck was about to change; worms were being crushed under my feet, so, I bent over and picked up a handful. I climbed back on the edge of the rock, quickly inserted one of the worms on the hook, and let it down into the clear, blue water. Also, I tossed some worms around the line that sank briskly. A whirlwind formed on the riverbed and stirred the water into the water current. Colonies of small, medium, and large fish bobbed one foot high in the air, hitting and nibbling on the bait.

I realized something was fishy; I tried to guess what was making the multitude of fish bob out of the water. The shape and color of the fish were strange. In fact, I had never seen these beautiful fish before. But I was happy now knowing I was going to catch many of them, and my holy grail was to put all of them in my fish bag, and I reasoned to myself, it was going to be a special gift for Zishe, and surely, Dr. Watters would forgive me.

Obviously, Joseph, the Wizard was observing me closely and having a good time. I didn't realize he was waiting for the precise time to put me and the fish in the same bag for eternity. This was to be a gift to his big boss, Thudil, the prince of the darker side of the entire universe, that he would enjoy till the end of time.

A multitude of fish started to chew the bait on the hook, and instantly, the whole colony began to bite and fight among themselves for the flesh. A long, fat fish, with honed blades on its tail, and a sword-edge nose kept swimming and cutting everything to pieces that was in its way. Finally, it stopped a few inches from the hook. It opened its red bulky pop-out eyes and detached them from its body. It rolled its eyes around like a pair of radar and attached them back to its body. It swam in slow motion, timing the action that it would take forthwith. Then it stung its own tongue, opened its mouth, and wrapped its tongue around again; the line was not touching the deadly, poisonous honed hook.

I felt the weight and pulling coming from the long line, and at once, saw a colorful, weird-looking fish. I was about to fall from the huge rock I was standing on because the force of the pull was so great. I got caught just in the nick of time, by a thick red net that landed over my head and trapped me. Instantly, it pulled, lifted me into the sky, and a witch transported me to the Weapons Den located on the tallest hill, where the deadliest, highest, and most dangerous waterfall was, and where Ed Tower had been offered some years before.

Eyewitnesses saw from surrounding towns, villages, and fields how I was enmeshed in a drift net, hovering in the air, and my body trapped inside. They also saw a queer-looking fish caught on the hook, and me grabbing the line, not willing to let it go. And the people on the ground screamed, chanted, and danced in jubilation, "That's a double catch!"

No one was aware that it was the son of their beloved Dr. Watters who had been caught, and that my life was in the hands of Joseph, the Wizard, and I would never be seen again. The word on the street, as always happened in the Saint

Nicholas Valley, was spreading rapidly and traveling at full speed. And within minutes, all the towns and villages' natives got together to find out if I had been the victim. They asked numerous questions among themselves. In a short time, Zishe heard the bad news, and a large number of natives went to take a peek into my room.

No one had the key because Dr. Watters had taken it with him so they couldn't check inside. And he was away visiting a patient that was dying in the neighboring village, called Philtekea Peak, the city known as "the School of Wizards or Bernard University." Zishe knew she didn't have much time, so she grabbed her sorcery rod, stroked it from end to end, and walked out the door without looking back.

She inspected every inch of the house quickly, shed a few tears in her bed, stared at the metal chest where I had hidden, and sealed the rat's tail that I had trapped. She lifted and stretched her rod toward the box and opened it; the tail moved and sent a yellow light in circles; Zishe understood that the tail was sending evil messages out. Immediately, she aimed her rod quickly at the lid and closed it before the tail could send more yellow warnings and green signals to alert Joseph, the Wizard, and Thudil.

Zishe took a quick trip to the toilet, and noticed fresh fingerprints, found one of my hairs, and a piece of my shirt, and she also examined my blood stain; she was sure it was the blood of the rat, not mine. She breathed fast, but she was sure she'd find me alive. She turned back to her room, and sat on her mysterious rocking chair, both hands on the rod; she looked up, then closed her eyes, and thought out the rescue mission.

I'M TORTURED

Joseph, the Wizard prepared all the tools he was going to use to punish me before he ripped my heart out to sacrifice it to the bloodthirsty Thudil. Leerd showed up and cut Joseph, The Wizard's powers, and informed him that Jus Supp wouldn't let him touch my soul. In other words, he and Thudil would not succeed in sending me to the grave yet. Leed's face faded away in Joseph, the Wizard's mind, and he started to feel pain; his legs were fleetingly crippled, and his evil brain's thoughts froze and failed to put his action plans together.

The same day, at the top of the hour, at exactly midnight, Joseph, the Wizard held an emergency meeting. He called all the lofty demons of all his soul-catcher factories to give them the heads up of a mandatory and urgent task that had to be completed by dawn. He gave them the master plan and instructions to carpenters, iron workers, weapon developers, welders, and all others, to work non-stop to create a new torture tool that same night, by six in the morning.

The ironworkers and the weapon builders came up with a dazzling proposal. All the demons present approved the plan that the builders had proposed; they approved it with a head nod. All the workers began to work, and in a few hours, they had built a long steel pole and a short one. I saw they had built a frightening bent and crook iron cross. They called Joseph, the Wizard to show him the finished deadly tool; he looked at me and saw my ashen face.

Joseph, the Wizard laughed and enjoyed seeing me soon-to-be hanging on the iron cross and roasting my flesh in the center of the infernal furnace. He thought that I was going to be barbecued until I lost every drop of blood to the infernal heat. He knew I wouldn't have a chance to be rescued, and eventually, my flesh would roast in the fire of the towering inferno.

ZISHE CALLED LEERD

Zishe didn't find a quick way to free me from the heat of the inferno Joseph, the Wizard had me in, and I was crucified on two pieces of tarnished metal. She called upon the goodness, the amazing grace, and glory of Jus Supp for help. Also, she knew she couldn't have an undisturbed chat with Jus Supp, so she needed to ask his son, Leerd, to come and help her.

Leerd heard and instantly answered by explaining to her that I must suffer for a little while to build the strength I needed to become the best air, land, and water fighter to defend goodness from the evil plots coming from Thudil. Jus Supp had chosen me to protect all his youngest children from Thudil setting them on fire, and from drowning them in the Pacific Ocean, soon. But I had to train hard and learn the hard way by suffering for a while.

Leerd blew a kiss to the sky, and soon a cloud formed in the middle of the blue sky; the smoke went up to heaven and knocked on heaven's door. The smoke was sent back down rapidly. Leerd zoomed all the clouds and stopped them ten feet away from Zishe's face. The clouds turned first into a large green screen, then blue, and lastly into a red, gigantic screen stained with drops of my blood, and burned, putrid flesh.

On the screen, amazing pictures appeared; some waterfalls falling three thousand feet, millions of droplets shooting from the clouds, and colossal trees showing their natural talents, jumping, swinging, and dancing in mid-air. My face was on top of the waterfall cliff, and two scary, muscular demons were handcuffed to me, one on each side. They had been handpicked to proceed with my torture ritual.

I was hanging on the iron cross, and a demon wearing a shako, and on fire was welding my arms on a bent horizontal beam, and a gnome demon was putting a metal ring on my shin to weld it to the long, crooked, vertical post. I moaned; the demons chanted, growing louder, sounding like thunderbolt storms. I was in such pain, and the whole area, including the demons, was turning into flames and fire.

Zishe closed her eyes, but in less than a second she opened them again, she blinked a couple of times to moisten them. She opened them wide, and rolled them, then she turned her face to the right where Leerd was standing; Zishe couldn't see him but felt his presence.

She opened her mouth and stuck out her tongue, but she closed her lips and tightened them. She wasn't able to pull back her tongue in time and hurt it, so, she was unable to speak for a good five minutes. She didn't have a choice but to wait and watch me being abused.

Leerd stopped the video for a second and sent signals to her brain to give her the heads up about my captivity. The good news was that Zishe learned that I was still alive and that all of her plans to free me would be carried out in the future, according to Leerd's decree. Leerd also explained to her that I should be tested with torture over, and over again, to train my mind to access the unknown and train my body to travel in diverse, dangerous galaxies. My body and spirit must be tormented for three months so I could learn to endure pain, educate my body to fight endless wars, protect the innocent, and punish the culpable ones, starting with Joseph, the Wizard, and all the evildoers that worked for Thudil, the Prince of Darkness.

The demons had just finished nailing me to the two pieces of iron, when Joseph, the Wizard shouted at the foot of the cross, "We are ready! Hang him high!" Lietie and Robtie, the two nasty demons chained to my wrists, wagged their tails in an affirmative reply. A few cut-off-tail demons brought two thin iron chains, locked one end to my right armpit, and the other one around my left. One strong, gigantic demon stamped his elephant feet on the ground that caused a tremor, and the demons jumped on top of his shoulders; he lifted the two demons that had been chosen to cut my body into small pieces, cook it, and hang it on the end of the iron bars as raw appetizers to view.

Joseph, the Wizard wrote down their mistakes, lowering Lietie to balance, as he was hanging on the left side of the scale. I looked at Robtie and asked him a few meaningless questions to increase my confidence because I was already crying and shaking, and in a panic. I needed to control my body and spirit.

Leerd played the video for Zishe to watch me for one more second and paused it again; Zishe's eyes were wet with tears because she was watching me live. He played it again in high-speed mode to show her all the torture methods Joseph, the Wizard had in store to try on my already mangled body; he revealed to her a frame of the last killing attempt, and how he was going to rescue me.

Leerd played the video on the screen for Zishe, but she covered her eyes because she thought she was going to faint. Leerd assured her that I was going to be fine. Leerd declared, "It is the last video you are going to watch." He gently rubbed her hand and removed it from Zishe's eyes, He pressed the start button, and played it.

Zishe smiled and took a deep breath, and said slowly and firmly, "I'll watch it." And she moved her lips in slow motion, "Thank you, Leerd, for showing me the rescue plans."

EPIDEMIC

Joseph, the Wizard had tried a ton of painful and deadly torture tools, but he hadn't been successful in killing me yet. Honestly, he hadn't even been able to cause real pain in my physical body or psyche, and my mind remained strong and active.

Thudil had been on the lookout since I was brought to the savage inferno den. He brought the iron cross burning in flames close to my face, with the two demons pinned to my sides. The torture show was a delight for the demons hanging next to me until they saw that I didn't melt in the inferno's heat ut they were burning to ashes. Joseph, the Wizard, and Thudil were gaping at the party going on in the middle of the eternal inferno. I was coming out of the burning cross alive, but the demons had been reduced to ashes. I was singing, laughing, and holding a colorful hose as I was showering water to keep myself safe from the heat, so the heat inside the inferno furnace didn't set me on fire.

Tudil ordered Joseph, the Wizard to find a dreadful technique to savagely kill me. Thudil spoke to his drudges that if they didn't sacrifice me, he would spread an epidemic on earth, and a fatal plague to exterminate demons and humans. The epidemic would finish off every moving creature. Men would try to find a magic cure and inject all kinds of chemicals into their bodies to ease the affliction, but nothing would work. Thudil assured them, the medicine they'll discover would never work, and the epidemic would never stop. Thudil also reminded them, wealthy people would profit from selling gadgets for people to cover their faces, and wrapping things, such as plastic gloves and covers on their arms and hands, but no matter what they'd do, it wouldn't stop the spreading of the bacteria and viruses. But at that moment, Leerd whispered to me, "In the end, I will meddle; I'll free you, and you will get superpowers to fight and eliminate the epidemic."

Meanwhile, Joseph, the wizard dug a hole and planted a dark artificial mushroom. The demons celebrated dancing around him; they were already celebrating and enjoying my flesh that they were going to peel off from my bones. Joseph planted a nuclear bomb next to the mushroom and he set the timer to explode in seventy-seven hours.

The mushroom commenced to root out in all directions under the dry, drab soil. Joseph, the Wizard's demons started to water the roots with a special yellowish fuel. Three demons carried the fuel from a lake source where the water was being turned into deadly toxic chemicals. The demons flew over the hills, and valleys in plastic bags filled with toxic light gasses.

Joseph stared at his watch, to read the time and count every second that went by, He flipped through the pages of the huge map booklet to the location. He knew he had to be right on every single detail for his plan of action to work.

DROWN MIKE NOW

All the demons chanted, "Drown Mike, drown him, drown him now!" I saw an old skinny, handicapped demon with a body shape of a seahorse; he had been picked to choose the torture tool, and he began coughing and falling on his walking cane. He tripped and fell, but he quickly tried hard to stand up by himself and keep his balance without his cane.

Suddenly, he said, "I'll choose to connect him to a fishing hook, then drop him in and out, and fishing him out ten thousand times, or even millions of times until he drowns, and breathes no more."

Joseph, the Wizard applauded the plan, and with a nod, he signaled his approval. Thudil shook his head, paused, nodded twice, raised his thumbs, and approved the plan just invented by The Hunch, as the Seahorse demon was known in the demons' kingdom.

Without delaying the punishment any further, Joseph, The Wizard carried out the plan and got ready to start the final torture, done to any mortal for the first time ever; I was about to be the first one picked up by the demons to be tortured and executed using that new execution technique. The question I asked myself was, "*Will Zishe come to help me?*" I hoped and prayed that the plan would fail. And I kept asking myself. *Are Zishe and Leerd aware of it, and will they keep watching out over the fishing area to wait for the right moment to rescue me?*"

Joseph, the Wizard moved fast to start the sacrificial ritual. In a second, he was ready to carry out the torture. He wrote on an Evergreen tree leaf and drew a map, and he pointed and marked the position where each demon soldier had to be positioned to secure the area as he was aware that Zishe and Leerd might show up and attack them to rescue me. Joseph knew the power Zishe had with her magic rod in her hand, and she might kill each one of his demons. And it will be a defeat that Thudil would never forget or forgive.

On the other hand, somewhere nearby, Zishe inspected her rod and practiced a little to make sure it worked, and she made sure she wouldn't miss a single shot.

She was expecting to move at any second to free me; in fact, she would attack when Leerd gave her the word to proceed. At that exact moment, the walls of her house should turn into a gigantic screen. And she would watch live what was going on at the pond. Thudil ordered speakers to be installed and pop up on every corner of homes' roofs, and radio announcers broadcasted live for all humanity to listen to the best ritual event performed since the creation of the world.

Thudil had a master plan for the ritual act and demanded Joseph, the Wizard to be sharp and unique, and he had made a mandatory publication to all demons to make sure it was broadcasted, watched, and heard everywhere in his territory. Speakers were installed everywhere, in all houses that were built and still standing all over the planet and beyond. The demons spread-out all-over Saint Nicholas Valley and mounted a big screen on every rooftop. Speakers carried out sounds of loud scary screams, and maniacal voices were heard as the devils were getting ready for the execution.

I was tied to a tall tree guarded by a multitude of demons since I had already been taken down from the two-rail bar cross and tied to a tree branch with their long tails, to make sure no feral beast approached and dared to loosen me to eat me. Because Joseph, the Wizard knew this was not only his first chance, but his only one, and one to put me to sleep for good, he had extra security protection everywhere.

By now, Zishe was watching on the walls that had turned into screens, and she was sketching to come up with a good rescue sketch map. Her eyes were creating two thin and curved rivers of tears. All kinds of animals swam across to come help and support her. They all sang a song dedicated to me, and birds flew over the house in a formation of three patterns of stars. One kind of bird formed the blue star formation, the second formation was a white star, and the third formation created a green star. All the animals encouraged Zishe to fight to the end.

The evil radio announcer broadcasted and said in a few distorted sentences "I have the honor to put a stop to any ongoing program in the kingdom to announce to our favorite fans, listeners, and supporters the event of the century; it'll never be heard or seen again. Today Mike Watters will be sacrificed, and the kingdom of Thudil will take over complete control. Darkness will rule over light, and nights will replace days," He went on, "And this is the new motto: 'Do Not Judge Me by My Shadow;' translation, the ones that seek the light or disobey me, will be severely tortured, and brought to book."

Good people hurried to spread the rumors that now was the end of times. Bad folks who were the majority of the planet's population, welcomed the new era and the rules of the dark times of Thudil. And they cheered Joseph, the Wizard, and his demons. They were happy, so happy attacking each other, and the killing among themselves went through the roof. That was the beginning of hate; same-sex, nasty orgies, bestiality, killing, famines, and demon worship was mandatory for all citizens of the land.

Zishe was pacing and crying; she looked feeble and pale as she sat on her rocking chair. She gripped her staff with her right hand and stretched it out and pointed to the door. It opened for her to look at the blue sky, birds, butterflies, bugs, insects, and all kinds of heavenly flying creatures passing by in the sky; she was glad to see their amazing wings moving at a marked pace, almost like marching in perfect formation. All of a sudden, from the very top of heaven, a window opened, a tiny dot dropped, and it descended at a slow speed. Then it sped up and came down with the speed of light. It halted about fifty-five feet from Zishe's door, and it kept hovering.

At that instant, an eagle-man was levitating, one who she had never seen in her entire life; the strange creature was waving at her; she dropped her rod, and quickly bent down for a second to pick it up. She raised her head again, but the human eagle had vanished. She aimed the rod at the door to close it. A mysterious note was at the door, and it read: "A Friend of Mike.

"I met him at the pond, on the bank of Saint Nicholas River some time ago, the same spot Mike loves to go fishing. Thudil and Joseph, the Wizard has everything ready for Mike's soul sacrifice. And I heard Thudil yell, 'I want his heart fresh just as you gave me Eddy Tower's heart some time ago. Oh, lad, that flesh was juicy, yummy, and tasty!'

Leerd and Ruddy the Eagle-man had the last meeting to review the rescue mission in charge of Ruddy, the Eagle-man. Leerd gave him the last-minute instructions and instructed him on the movements and directions for the fatal rescue dive.

He finished with, 'You became the Eagle-man to die rescuing Mike and prepare the way for him to become the greatest superhero that ever lived. Soon, he will be called MegAm and he will always honor and remember your name.'"

I had been pinned to a fishing hook that the Hunch demon had built from a tree's skinny metal chain, a thick, old one, a rusty hook, and a dusty long cable. I hung ten feet from the water, head down because they had chained my ankles to tie the iron hook in between my legs. The ceremony began, and it was supposed to be over in a minute, Joseph, the Wizard began the countdown from five to zero, and the torture started. I was dropped one time, two, three… and the demons held my body in the air to mock me. The Hunch demon gave the orders to swing me up slowly, and then swing me down quickly.

I heard a voice whisper in my ear, "I'm coming to rescue you; I already know I'm going to die in three days for rescuing you, but it's my mission. Leerd chose me to save you from Joseph, the Wizard's evil plots."

Joseph, the Wizard heard Ruddy, the Eagle-man whispering to me. A minute of silence came, nothing moved, nobody spoke or moved; suddenly Joseph, the Wizard laughed at the top of his lungs, and said, "The party must go on!" I was tossed like a mallet down into the water that splashed and elevated about ten feet into the air in the shape of an umbrella. The last time I was pulled out of the water, I was choking to death, so I was given a quick breathing break. The Hunch demon started swinging me up doing loops and sinking just my head to my neck when I hit the water. A flock of white birds came down and flew high, then dove landing on the pond, singing especially for me, and started building a tall funnel with their formation going up. The bird tunnel reached the clouds and went all the way to heaven's window, which Zishe had seen a few minutes ago on the screen.

The birds kept hovering, holding their position, as if they were guarding the stairway to heaven. Joseph, the Wizard just looked; all of a sudden, Ruddy the Eagle-man fell in a deadly dive, coming from heaven's door, and grabbed me, then he pulled hard so that The Hunch demon, who was holding the pole, was jerked down into the water.

The Eagle-man stopped in the air, and holding me tightly, he lifted me. He swathed me with his half-eagle-man legs, and he jumped to slap Joseph, the Wizard's face with his sharp claws. The Eagle-man dove and swam underneath the water; he untied me and flew away into the birds' tunnel.

Minutes later, Zishe heard a pounding at the door. She gripped her wand firmly, and pointed it at the door, ready to fire hailstone fire.

Leerd's voice blared in her ears, "Don't shoot! I bring you good news." She opened the door and saw me; my body was bruised, dirty, and wounded. She noticed that my heart was pounding irregularly, and I couldn't take a single step on my own. A man with an eagle's claws, a head, and a nose long as an eagle's bill, the arms of a bird, and a human body covered with an eagle's feathers was holding me from behind.

The Eagle-man brought me inside. Zishe called Dr. Watters who was busy working in his lab. She informed him to come urgently to give me treatment and briefed him that I was back home.

The Eagle-man told Zishe the rescue story in a few sentences and went back to heaven where he was scheduled to dwell in three days.

RUDDY, THE EAGLE-MAN TAKEN

And here was an untold story; Ruddy, the Eagle-man was sad, and started pacing on Saint Nicholas River's edge. Three days after he had rescued me. I was already there trying to catch a fish for Zishe. I had been sitting on my favorite rock for a long time and had caught nothing. Ruddy, the Eagle-man came and stood next to me; he suggested I cast my small fishing net to the left; the net moved down very slowly, and my eyes were peeled and grew so big, that they seemed to pop out of their sockets.

Ruddy the Eagle-man stared at me and said in a gentle voice, "What's happening to you, Pop Eye?" I touched my eyes, and scute plates came out of one of them.

The school of fish quickly swam away from me, and they sank into the deep waters and pulled Ruddy, the Eagle-man into the deep waters because he was not standing firmly on the ground. Before he touched the riverbed, he turned into the Eagle-man; he swam up and used the current as a runway for twenty feet, and then he took off. I noticed how he soared up in the sky with the net filled with fish trying to get out underneath him. Ruddy, the Eagle-man disappeared over the clouds.

I rubbed my eyes, lowered my face, and picked up the line of my fishing rod to toss and hoped to catch some fish. Ruddy, the Eagle-man was gone; I went back to fishing, and Ruddy, the Eagle-man dropped a large fish on purpose; it fell from the sky vertically, sliding from the end of the line, sank and bit the hook, and got caught in it. I had to use all my skills to hold the rod tightly, nevertheless, I lost my grip, and the fishing rod went flying in the air. Luckily, it got stuck in between a dead tree log and a stationary rock. I looked up and saw the acrobatic Eagle-man coming down, piercing the dark cloud.

In a second, he was hanging in front of me, hovering ten feet above the water, and the net five feet from touching the water. He waved me goodbye and went up, and he flew away again. From the clouds,

I heard Ruddy, the Eagleman saying, "I fought to protect you from the satanic forces of Joseph, the Wizard, even when I belong in heaven, I would help you."

I pulled out the fishing rod with a huge three-pound fish caught on the hook. A couple of minutes later, Ruddy, the Eagle-man was gone, and as soon as he landed on his ranch, he was transformed into his human form.

That day, I came back soon because I had caught a shoal of fish in a flash, I mean Ruddy, the Eagle-man had given me the net filled to the brim with fish. Ruddy, the Eagle-man had also headed home with a bag of fish on his shoulders. He was about twenty feet from the door when he heard moaning, so he stopped and listened carefully. He heard a familiar voice inside. He had told his wife he'd be back late in the afternoon, but, he had returned early. He opened the door slowly and went in and saw his wife having sex; he grabbed his knife and got ready to attack the intruder. He raised his hand high to stab them both at the same time as the knife was long, thin, and sharp. Suddenly, a strange beam of fire shone through his hand, melted the knife, and reduced it to dust. The ashes fell on Joseph, the Wizard's naked body.

Ruddy, the Eagle-man, hurled himself forward to wrestle Joseph, the Wizard to death. Joseph scooted to his left, and Ruddy, the Eagle-man landed on his wife and squashed her naked body, breaking four of her ribs. His wife just moaned in pain. Joseph, the Wizard had enough time to grab one of his knives from his belt collection. He took a few steps back and chose the corner to keep a distance to avoid wrestling Ruddy, the Eagle-man since he knew he wasn't a match for him in a wrestling match.

He licked the blade's tip, aimed it at his heart, and threw it to kill; Ruddy, the Eagle-man leaned to the right side as fast as his tired legs could respond. The blade went flying past and he got pinned to the wall. Ruddy, the Eagle-man felt hot blood running down his left cheek. He wiped it and spit out saliva mixed with blood. A second golden blade was flashing, flying, and whistling close to his ears. He jumped up to the tile ceiling. His wife yelled in panic on seeing him turning into Eagle-man on the way up because she wasn't aware that her husband had this superpower.

Ruddy, the Eagle-man attached his long bill and his claws to the ceiling and hung like a bat. Joseph, the Wizard's army stormed inside the house, firing from every direction at the batman who was walking on the ceiling. The Eagle-man was cornered in his own home; by this time an army of demons was attacking him; he didn't have a chance to flee or come out alive. He was wounded, and a couple of bullets were burning into one of his legs. His own wife was watching him die.

Joseph, the Wizard was loading his most powerful gun with a special silver bullet. Ruddy, the Eagle-man banged his head to open up a hole and bolt for freedom through the roof; tile pieces fell on the floor. He looked up at the blue sky where he had traveled freely, multiple times. Many times, he'd had the gift of flying with ease as an eagle-man, but now it was about to end his happy times at the Saint Nicholas green valley.

He shouted at the top of his lungs, "Finally, I am going to be with you for eternity. Take care of Mike Watters!"

Joseph, the Wizard scratched his nose with his middle finger, brought it down to fit on the trigger, and looking at Ruddy, the Eagle-man's wife, blew her a kiss and turned to the ceiling. He fired the single bullet that hit Ruddy, the Eagle-man in the heart. A powerful heavenly force kept blowing in the wind, and slowly let Ruddy, the Eagle-man down, lowered his body, and gently placed him on the ground floor. Ruddy, the Eagle-man turned back into Ruddy the mortal man.

His wife, and Joseph, the Wizard heard the last words coming from Ruddy's dead body, "Mike Watters, AKA, MegAm."

Eyewitnesses certified and testified that a gigantic eagle with human legs and arms had been seen rescuing people, and fighting the evil Joseph, the Wizard. And every single time he wrote a yellow inscription, 'MegAm' in the sky

SOS MEN

Three months after Ruddy, the Eagle-man miraculously rescued me, I came out of hiding for the first time. Dr. Watters had snapped up an old white jeep about a year before. One evening at 7.03 I'd had a long conversation with him. He asked me to help him drive the jeep to take a trip to Sun City to go get more first aid supplies that he desperately needed. A new, rare, and highly contagious virus had been spreading fast. It had killed around eleven thousand people in a week. No one knew where it came from, and no known vaccine or medicine was available to cure it yet. The next day, I got up at five in the morning, got dressed in a flash, and at about 6.33 AM, Dr. Watters started up the engine; ten minutes later, he was driving in the mud; the driving was going to be about three hours and fifteen minutes one way because it was the rainy season, and the dirt road was very slippery and swampy. In this season, most of the roads were muddy and slippery. The small bridges were flooded, in fact, it was risky driving. Dr. Watters had already driven about forty-five minutes when he realized he had forgotten the list of medical items. He didn't have a choice but to turn around and go back home to get it.

At ten, when he was driving up the steep mountain, the jeep started overheating; he had no choice but to stop to let the engine cool off for a minute. I stood on the side, under a big Oak tree for shade.

Twenty-five minutes had gone by, and he was back on the road again. Indeed, in a few minutes, Dr. Watters reached the peak and started to descend the mountain; in the distance, he was looking at the tall buildings in downtown Sun City. We were exhausted. The rain was very heavy; it was pouring on our soaked bodies as the jeep didn't have a roof. Because the soil was fragile, a tree was uprooted and had fallen from the hill and blocked the road on a dangerous bend. Another tree rolled down about a hundred feet and landed on the highway. We were lucky that the tree hit the ground three feet behind the jeep. If we had been a split second later, the gigantic tree would have landed on top of us. We and the jeep would have been ground to dust and buried alive underneath the lava, and the wet soil, rocks, and tree would have fallen on us. We wouldn't have been able to escape or survive. We heard a bomb blast and stood still for a second. Dr. Watters turned around and said a quick prayer to thank Lord Jus Supp, God of Zishe, for saving us. He felt relaxed and continued driving down the steep hill after going around the fallen trees.

I was humming the tune to the last song I was arranging; that's all I could do. A branch was cut from a tall tree and came flying through the air. I saw the shadow, and I yelled at Dr. Watters to step on the gas pedal to avoid the wooden beam smashing and killing us instantly. Because Dr. Watters had sharp hearing, he heard the voice of a familiar man. He was right, it was Joseph, the Wizard climbing down the tree in a hurry. He was cursing the entire world for he had missed the target, and he was on the run to save his skin. Dr. Watters sped away for three minutes breathing heavily; finally. he stepped on the brake to slow down.

He looked back through the rear-view mirror and saw Joseph, the Wizard, and his men firing gunshots at us from far away, but he realized the bullets wouldn't hit us anymore, but Joseph, the Wizard was trying to scare us.

We crossed the last stream bridge, and we were two hundred feet short of getting onto the paved road, and about seven minutes of reaching the outskirts of Sun City.

Suddenly, Dr. Watters started shivering, so he asked himself a couple of questions. *What's happening to me? Is someone other than Joseph, the Wizard gaslighting me?* He answered his own question: *No, I don't think so, because I felt a good vibe, I mean it's a good spirit coming to protect us.* He stepped on the brakes again, and the instant he did that, the jeep came to a complete stop and ended in the middle of the highway, blocking the heavy traffic. A big cane-carrier truck driver slammed on brakes, stopped for a second, gave me the middle finger, then blasted the horn, drove around us, and sped away.

I saw him ahead of us; he stopped completely across the road, blocking the highway deliberately. He slapped himself on the cheeks to wake up for he had no idea that he was blocking the street. Immediately, he pushed down on the gas pedal, all the way to the floor, to escape, but the jeep that was in front of him didn't move an inch. He panicked as he didn't know what to do next. He buried his face in his hands and banged it on the steering wheel for thirty-three seconds.

He heard some voices coming from three different directions around the truck; they whistled in harmony. One had a hoarse sound, the other one was a shrill sound, and the third was in a bass voice.

I reacted and moved slightly to the left. I opened my eyes and looked around, to the right, then to the left, and then slid to the front. I saw three strange creatures radiant as the sun itself, standing there. Their bodies looked like they were made of golden curium.

A voice coming from the mountains was heard all over the valley, "I am Lord Jus Supp. My son, Mike Watters, will be taken by the SOS messengers on a training mission. He will return soon, and he will come down to liberate the children of the world."

The voice stopped, and I was escorted to the center of the road by one of the three men in yellow and stood on the center line. The three men gathered around me, and vehicles ran over us, but they went through our bodies; the men were holding hands and forming a circle to protect me as I was hypnotized. They spoke in code, and I repeated the words in code. A golden beam of light descended from the sun and formed a funnel at the tip of the beam, sucked me in, and transported me together with the Sons of Sun, to the center of the sun.

Within minutes, Sun City's main radio station breaking news broadcasted the still-unknown event. Cable TV and newspapers posted pictures of the abandoned jeep. An inscription on the windshield read: "SOS (Sons of Sun) will be back soon after training and conferring on Mike Watters his superhero name of 'MegAm'"

Dr. Watters heard the news; he was in the middle of the road in the driver's seat, searching for a way to start up the jeep. Sadly, back in Zishe's room, she had already died before I returned vested with the name of MegAm and a yellow superhero suit, with the face of an Eagle-man printed on the back of the suit, in memory of Rudy, the Eagle-man. She never got the chance to see me alive again; she had waited every afternoon as she wanted just to see me one last time poking my face into her room, but it never became reality. Although she knew Lord Jus Supp had chosen me to save the world, and I was in training somewhere in a distant unknown galaxy because I had been taken by the yellow SOS messengers to learn the code, learn flying, make wise choices in aerodynamics, and to fit me in a fancy yellow superhero suit. Before she died, Zishe left her wand locked in a rusty old, long, rectangular metal box with a code written on it: To be opened by Mike because he is the only one chosen to break the combination code. She wrote the code on top of the box. But before she sealed the box, she placed a note wrapped around the wand, inside the box:

And when Mike has run
All the way down, a free fall from the sun
I was long gone for fun
I left my wand, and a code, a chess dun.

Immediately, I sat lost in thought, calling Zishe out loud; she didn't prattle nowadays. I opened the chest, took the wand, and was ready to fight evil.

www.ingramcontent.com/pod-product-compliance
Lightning Source LLC
Chambersburg PA
CBHW071602180626
46817CB00013B/1259